"Melissa, calm down," Will said. "Maybe we should go outside. We can find somewhere to talk." He reached out a hand to her, but she knocked it away.

"I don't want to go outside," she said through clenched teeth, no longer aware of the crowd or the music or the heat. All she could see was Will's steadily paling face. "How long?" she asked. "How long have you been planning to dump me?"

There was an audible gasp from the spectator circle. Melissa barely noticed. "Melissa, please," Will said. "You don't want to do this."

"How long?" Melissa shouted, the tears brimming over.

Will didn't answer—he just stood there staring at her, all concerned and pitying. He felt bad for her. How sweet. He felt bad that she was standing in the middle of a crowded room, crumbling like a bag of potato chips, all because he'd broken her heart.

Hold it together, Melissa told herself. *Just get out of here and everything will be . . . will be . . .* But she couldn't finish the sentence. Everything was not going to be fine. Ever.

Don't miss any of the books in SWEET VALLEY HIGH
SENIOR YEAR, an exciting new series from Bantam Books!

#1 CAN'T STAY AWAY
#2 SAY IT TO MY FACE
#3 SO COOL
#4 I'VE GOT A SECRET
#5 IF YOU ONLY KNEW
#6 YOUR BASIC NIGHTMARE

Visit the Official Sweet Valley Web Site on the Internet at:

http://www.sweetvalley.com

Francine Pascal's

SVH senioryear

Your Basic Nightmare

CREATED BY
FRANCINE PASCAL

BANTAM BOOKS
NEW YORK · TORONTO · LONDON · SYDNEY · AUCKLAND

RL 6, age 12 and up

YOUR BASIC NIGHTMARE
A Bantam Book / July 1999

Sweet Valley High® is a registered trademark of Francine Pascal.
Conceived by Francine Pascal.
Cover photography by Michael Segal.

Produced by 17th Street Productions,
a division of Daniel Weiss Associates, Inc.
33 West 17th Street
New York, NY 10011.

ISBN: 0-553-48612-8

Published simultaneously in the United States and Canada

*Bantam Books are published by Bantam Books, a division of Random
House, Inc. Its trademark, consisting of the words "Bantam Books" and
the portrayal of a rooster, is Registered in U.S. Patent and Trademark
Office and in other countries. Marca Registrada. Bantam Books, 1540
Broadway, New York, New York 10036.*

PRINTED IN THE UNITED STATES OF AMERICA

OPM   0 9 8 7 6 5 4 3 2 1

To Valentine

Will Simmons

Here's the lesson for the day: Never make promises.

I'm not talking about little ones like promising your kid sister you'll take her to see Barney on Ice or promising your mom you'll mow the lawn. I'm talking about those other promises. The ones you make in the heat of the moment. The ones you make under delusions of love. The ones some people think of as written in blood.

I promised Melissa I would never leave her. And I meant it. I was in eighth grade. I was a kid. But I knew at that moment that I would never love anyone else. And I knew that Melissa needed me and that I could be there for her no matter what.

I had no idea what I was in for.

Ken Matthews

To: mslater@swiftnet.com
From: kenQB@swiftnet.com
Time: 8:04 pm
Subject: Liz & Conner

Maria—

   Have you talked to Liz yet? Let me know if you need to spill. I'll be around.

                                        —Ken

Conner McDermott

I <u>really</u> want Liz.

There. I said it. When I kissed her in the hall . . . I'll just say this, I never knew a kiss could feel like that. And I've kissed a lot of girls. Trust me.

The thing is, right now I don't know what to do. (Yes, I'm admitting it.) I know I can't do the whole relationship thing. Never been good at it. And I know that's what Elizabeth wants. Elizabeth Wakefield is definitely the deep-relationship type.

So what do I do?

No. Seriously. I'm asking.

What do I do?

Disorientation

1

Not right. This is not right. This is just not right.

Jeremy Aames was in serious denial as he followed his mother out of the parking structure toward the well-lit hospital entrance. They didn't speak. They had barely spoken since she picked him up—no, intercepted him—at Trent's party. She had pulled up outside Trent's house just as Jeremy was chasing after Jessica Wakefield, his very distraught date.

Now, as they passed through the big, sliding-glass door into the harsh fluorescent lighting of Joshua Fowler Memorial Hospital, Jessica had been nearly forgotten—at least temporarily pushed way to the back of his mind. Jeremy looked around the buzzing emergency room. Suddenly the world was all so sterile and so very wrong. His dad wasn't old; he was barely fifty—too young to have had a heart attack. He shouldn't be here. He should be home with his family.

Family.

"Mom," he called as she turned the corner ahead

of him. "Mom," he repeated. "Where are Trisha and Emma?"

"I sent your sisters next door to the Chapmans'," his mom called over her shoulder without breaking her stride.

Jeremy breathed a sigh of relief. At least his sisters were hanging out with a family friend—being kept away from all the drama.

How could this have happened? Jeremy gritted his teeth and silently followed his mother as she made a quick left, another left, and pushed through a set of double doors. His mom knew exactly where she was going, and she was power walking in a business suit and heels down a labyrinth of corridors.

Jeremy just blindly followed her, his heart racing. Suddenly the hallway opened up into a wider area, and then they were at a desk. The sign on the wall read Intensive Care Unit.

Intensive care. Jeremy swallowed hard.

His mother struggled to catch her breath. "My husband?"

The middle-aged nurse behind the counter looked up from a chart. "Can I help you?" she asked.

"I'm Margaret Aames. How is my husband? He's supposed to be up here. How is he?"

Jeremy felt his pulse quicken. His mother was babbling. She never babbled. What if his father was in serious danger? What if he was going to . . . to die?

The nurse pulled out a clipboard and glanced

2

over a chart covered with scribbles. "There has been no change," the nurse said softly. "But that's not necessarily bad at this point. He's stable."

"Stable is good?" Mrs. Aames asked, her voice wavering slightly. It broke Jeremy's heart.

"Stable is good," the nurse assured her. She came out from behind the desk and smiled at Jeremy. "This must be your son."

"I'm Jeremy," he said.

"It's nice to meet you," she responded. Her voice was very soothing. "Come along with me, and we'll all look in on your father."

Jeremy took a deep breath and trailed behind his mother and the nurse, trying to quell the nausea that was building in his stomach.

"What happens next?" Jeremy blurted out. "When can he come home?" *Please say he's coming home.*

The nurse stopped at an open doorway and turned around. "You're going to have to talk to the doctor about that, but they'll monitor him here at the hospital for a bit." She looked up at Jeremy. He felt like she was monitoring him, making sure he was processing the information.

"Can we see him now?" Jeremy asked.

The nurse peeked inside the small room. "In a moment," she said. "One of the cardiothoracic attendings is finishing up with him right now. I'll pull aside the curtain when it's okay for you two to come in. You can have a seat over there or—"

"I'll stand," Jeremy said.

The nurse nodded, squeezed Mrs. Aames's arm consolingly, and disappeared into the ICU room.

Jeremy helped his mom into a chair. "You sit. I'll let you know when she comes back. He'll be okay, Mom." Mrs. Aames managed a tight smile.

Jeremy turned back to the doorway, watching the nurse's shadow as she talked with someone behind the curtain. He felt helpless. He already detested the intensive care unit, with its sour antiseptic smell, long corridors, and beeping sounds coming from all corners.

The nurse pulled back the curtain, and Jeremy froze. He felt the blood drain from his face. His dad lay there, totally still, hooked up to a lot of machines. A *lot* of machines.

"Mom?" Jeremy said. His mother jumped out of her chair and rushed through the doorway to his father's bedside. Jeremy inched his way into the room and hung back near the door, feeling scared and out of place.

Ever since Jeremy's father had been squeezed out of his lucrative VP position at a local computer company, he'd been depressed and lethargic, but trying to put on a brave front. Images of his father from the last year flashed through Jeremy's mind. Sifting through want ads, scouring his Rolodex for connections, searching Internet job sites. Early on, his father would go to interviews and get all excited about a potential job, but then he'd never mention it again. Lately things had been growing worse. Jeremy and his mother had been scrambling to pay bills while his father withdrew further and further.

I knew this was going to happen, Jeremy thought. His father had tried to keep his family from understanding how serious their financial situation had become. He had refused to share the burden until it was too late. Until he'd lost all hope and begun to slide.

"I wish there was something I could have done," Jeremy whispered. As he said the words, Jeremy realized that there *was* something he could do now. He'd make sure that from now on, his father's life was stress-free. He was going to be there for his father, no matter what.

Elizabeth Wakefield woke up, confused.

This is not my bed. This is not my comforter.

Everything came back to her instantly and in a rush. Even after weeks of living at the Sandborns' house, waking up in a strange room could still be disorienting.

Then she heard loud guitar music pulsing through the wall behind her headboard, and there was no mistaking her locale.

"Conner," she whispered, seeing his brilliant green eyes as she closed her own. She smiled.

Elizabeth had it bad.

Her mind conjured up an image of herself and Conner, standing outside their creative-writing classroom, staring into each other's eyes. She remembered the way he'd gently touched her face, the world fading out of focus, and the insistent pressure of his lips against hers. Elizabeth grinned and pulled the white comforter over her head. Was it possible? Had she and Conner really shared that very passionate, very public kiss?

She heard water running in the sink. Conner was in the bathroom that connected his room with hers. Suddenly Elizabeth's spirits waned. What the heck was she supposed to do now?

She was *living* with him. What was she going to do when she saw him? What would *he* do? This was the most ridiculous living situation Elizabeth had ever heard of. Two people, completely unsure of their relationship status, sharing a bathroom. Elizabeth burrowed further under the covers. One thing was for sure, Conner wouldn't be seeing her until she had a chance to shower.

It was mornings like this that made Elizabeth miss living with her sister. At least when she shared a bathroom with Jessica, she'd never been afraid to leave her room. Well, maybe for a week or two back in junior high, but she and Jessica were much more mature now.

Elizabeth heard an insistent scratching and realized Conner was brushing his teeth. She couldn't believe she could hear his every move.

"Ugh!" Elizabeth groaned. She folded up her pillow on either side of her head, smothering her ears. Suddenly she felt a pulling at her neck. Her necklace had gotten snagged on the piping at the hem of the pillowcase.

"Oh, no," Elizabeth said, a moment before she heard the snap. She pulled the pillow away and gasped. The stylish chain Maria had given her on her last birthday hung from the edge of the pillowcase.

Elizabeth started fussing with the necklace, trying to detach it without doing any more damage.

"Maria's going to kill me," Elizabeth whimpered. But even as she inspected the chain, she knew Maria would never care about the necklace . . . once she found out about Elizabeth and Conner. Then she would *really* kill Elizabeth.

She'd broken the golden rule. She'd kissed the guy her best friend loved. Even though Conner had dumped Maria pretty harshly, Maria was still hung up on him. And had Elizabeth comforted her friend—offered advice? A bit. But mostly Elizabeth had been too busy lying about her own feelings and sneaking around behind Maria's back.

Elizabeth put the broken necklace down on her bedside table and grabbed the phone. Feeling guilty about Maria always gave Elizabeth the urge to talk to her. It was as if she needed to prove Maria was still there, not hating her. Maybe she would be up for brunch or something.

7

Maria picked up on the third ring.

"Hey, you," Elizabeth said.

"Hey, Liz," Maria responded in a flat voice.

Elizabeth blinked. Was Maria being chilly to her? "What's wrong?"

"Nothing," Maria said, still tone-free.

"Are you sure?" Why was she pressing? Did she really want to hear Maria bring up the obvious reason she was bummed? It was Conner. It was *always* Conner. And Elizabeth just didn't want to have to talk with Maria about him right now. It took too much out of her. Besides, she wanted to focus on the happy.

"Well, there is something," Maria said. "A big something."

What kind of big something? Elizabeth worried. *Oh God. Did she see us? Did she see us kiss?*

"How big?" Elizabeth asked apprehensively.

Maria took a deep breath. "Really big." She paused. "A big, huge, monster zit."

Elizabeth closed her eyes and quietly sighed in relief.

"Right next to my ear," Maria continued. "It's awful. It's huge. I'm a leper."

"I'm sure it's not that bad," Elizabeth assured her.

"It *is* that bad. I'm not leaving my house for five days."

"But then who will I go out for brunch with?" Elizabeth asked.

"Today?" Maria exclaimed. "You want me to go out today? Have you not been listening? I might as well have smallpox."

Elizabeth laughed. "Maria, smallpox was eradicated. We just learned that in history, remember?"

"Yeah, well, Mrs. Rothman had her facts wrong."

"Hey, Maria?"

"Yeah?"

"I just used an SAT word. *Eradicate*. You're it."

Maria sighed. "I hate this game. Too much pressure."

Elizabeth stood up and detangled the telephone cord as she crossed the room to her windows. She flung open the curtains to reveal a beautiful, sunny day. "Yeah, well, you're the one who wants to go to Yale," she said. "So, do you want to eat or not? I have a coupon for the Eggshell. You know you love their chocolate-chip pancakes."

Conner's bedroom door slammed, and Elizabeth's senses went on alert. She whirled around and stared at her closed bedroom door as if she could see right through it. Then she pulled down on her flannel nightshirt as if he could see her too.

"All right. You talked me into it. Who has the Jeep?" Maria asked.

Elizabeth heard Conner barreling down the steps.

"What? Oh. It's Jessica's week. Can you pick me up?"

The front door closed. Elizabeth listened for the

sound of the Mustang starting up in the driveway. Nothing. What was he doing?

"Sure," Maria said. "But I don't want to come in. I don't want to see him. Okay?"

Elizabeth's attention snapped back to Maria. "Um, it's okay," she said. "I think he just left."

"I don't want to risk it," Maria said.

"Okay," Elizabeth said, noting the bitter tone in her friend's voice. "I'll meet you out front."

"I'll honk," Maria said. "Is fifteen minutes okay?"

"Make it half an hour," Elizabeth said. "I'll still have to take the world's quickest shower."

"Well, get on it. Make it the Guinness world record for getting ready. I'll see you soon."

"Bye, Maria."

Elizabeth rushed out into the hall and down to the windows that faced the front yard. Conner's car was in the driveway. She pressed her face to the glass so she could see more of the lawn. He wasn't doing yard work. Maybe he was in the garage or something. Or maybe he'd walked over to Tia's. Whatever the case, there was no way of telling when he was going to show up again. Elizabeth hurried back to the bathroom.

"Please don't let him come home," she muttered as she turned on the water in the shower full force. "If I have to see him and Maria at the same time, I'm definitely going to have a nervous breakdown."

*   *   *

"What a beautiful southern California morning," the deejay singsonged on the radio. "From Los Angeles to San Diego, not a cloud in the sky!"

Jessica Wakefield groaned. She threw one pillow at her clock radio and buried her head under another. Unfortunately the radio was stronger than the pillow.

"And this morning the Laguna Beach 5K Race for the Cure is already under way to raise money for breast cancer research," the deejay continued. "Last week's race in Sweet Valley raised—"

Jessica threw her other pillow at the radio. Not that she was against charity or anything; it was just too early for noise of any kind—well-intentioned or not. She covered her eyes against the sunlight streaming through the window, wondering why she never remembered to shut the blinds at night. The radio blared on, announcing the day's big events.

"Don't forget the big Sweet Valley High football game against Pueblo Valley," Jessica said bitterly. "The one I'm suspended from. No game, no friends, no boyfriend . . . beautiful morning, my butt!"

Jessica sighed and sat up, squinting against the light. Her eyes hurt, so she closed them again. She had been up most of the night, crying. Never in her life had she felt so beaten. Not only had Melissa and her we-hate-Jessica bandwagoners totally destroyed Jessica's reputation, but Jeremy—cute, fun, thoughtful Jeremy—had seemingly written her off.

11

Jessica groaned and opened her eyes, catching a glimpse of herself in the big, beveled mirror across from her bed. Her blond hair looked more like a rat's nest than a smart, chin-length cut. She pushed the mop back from her face, rubbed her eyes, and stretched, making a small squeaking sound before she flopped backward. Unfortunately her pillows were somewhere in the vicinity of the radio and she landed with a thud against the firm mattress.

She was just contemplating going back to sleep, pillowless and all, when the phone rang. Jessica's heart jumped. "It's not for you," she chastised herself.

It rang again, and Jessica pursed her lips. Okay. There was a *slim* possibility it could be for her. Maybe . . . Jessica sprang out of bed and opened her door a crack. If it was for her, the Fowlers' butler, Eduardo, would come up the stairs to let her know.

Please let it be Jeremy. Please. Please. Please.

She peered down the hall. Eduardo was a no-show. Jessica closed her door with a bang.

"Get a life," she muttered to herself. "Jeremy is not going to call."

Last night when Jeremy had picked her up for their first date, she had been full of hope and excitement. And she hadn't been disappointed. The party was amazing. Good food, incredible music, and above all, nice people. It had been a long time since Jessica had been in the company of so many nice people.

She had almost felt like her old self again—chatting with different groups and attracting admiring glances everywhere she went. She had felt comfortable again. Popular. Liked.

Until Melissa Fox and her two best buddies had shown up. Nothing like a little public humiliation to turn a guy off completely—even a sweet guy like Jeremy.

Jessica grabbed a pillow off the floor and flung it onto the bed. "Loser," she muttered.

It was going to be a lousy day. A bad-hair day for the record books—she could tell already. At least she didn't have to go to work. She wouldn't have to see Jeremy the day after he dumped her.

In fact, she never, ever, *ever* wanted to see him again. What kind of guy let his date run out of a party crying and didn't follow her? Even if she had just been called a slut in front of all his friends.

"Nope. I don't need him," Jessica said, perching on the edge of her bed. She looked at the closed bedroom door. Still, it would be nice if he called. . . .

I am a loser.

Jessica dragged herself into the bathroom and turned on the shower. She stared at her reflection in the mirror as the glass fogged over.

"One mistake. I am still paying for one little mistake," she said. Why had she ever kissed Will Simmons? Will—who stood by last night and let Jessica get ripped to shreds. Just stood there and did

13

nothing—as always. And why couldn't Melissa and her friends just drop it already? They'd won. Melissa had Will, and Jessica had nothing. When were they going to stop torturing her?

Jessica would give anything to stay in bed all day. To bury herself under her pillows and disappear completely. But no. She had to get dressed and go to her game. No, correction, not *her* game—she'd been suspended after missing the last game. After she'd run off when she thought Melissa and the rumor squad were going to tell Jeremy all about her fictional sordid past. But they hadn't told him then. They'd waited until last night—until they had a huge audience.

Still, it was going to be the sidelines for Jessica while everyone else cheered. Whatever. She was getting used to being on the sidelines.

Jeremy Aames

Nothing like a crossword puzzle to bore you even further out of your mind.

—7 *letters,* worn out, exhausted.

Haggard: *My mom looks haggard this morning, especially after this, her tenth cup of coffee.*

—4 *letters,* time unit.

Hour: *About how long I slept sitting in this damn hospital waiting room. Some way to spend a Friday night. I wish I could take a shower. What I wouldn't give right now for a shower.*

—6 *letters,* shackle.

Fetter: *Dr. Fetters says Dad has to take it easy. Isn't that ironic? Dad hasn't really done anything in a long time.*

—4 *letters,* unexcited, mellow.

Calm: *Dad is supposed to stay calm and rested. Meanwhile Mom and I go* crazy . . . and unshowered. I really, very much want a shower. Did I mention that?

—4 letters, philosophical prefix.

?: I don't know. Should I know this? I can't know everything. I can't do everything.

—4 letters, beautiful.

Jessica: Okay, okay, that's too many letters, but I'm going to try to squeeze it in anyway.

CHAPTER 2
Everything Happens for a Reason

Melissa Fox couldn't run fast enough.

It was gaining on her. She didn't know what it was—she couldn't see it or hear it. But she could feel it all around her. And whatever it was wanted her dead. It was determined to crush her.

Melissa tried to outrun it, but it was like running through water. Running through oatmeal. She stumbled and fell and couldn't get up again. Melissa was scrambling, clawing, groping. It was right on top of her. She opened her mouth to scream—

And her eyes flew open.

Melissa bolted upright in bed, her heart racing. *Oh my God. Oh my God.* Hand to chest, Melissa fought to calm her breathing.

Her eyes darted first to the phone and then to the clock. It was 10 A.M. When had she fallen asleep? And had the phone really remained silent? Could it be that Will actually hadn't called? Melissa reached over and picked up the receiver on her blue Princess phone. The dial tone was humming away.

"I don't believe this," Melissa whispered, placing

the phone back in its cradle. She closed her eyes and leaned back into her pillows, hearing Will's words in her mind.

Call off your attack dogs. . . . I swear if you don't go over there right now, I'm outta here.

And he'd actually left. He'd left Melissa, Cherie, and Gina stranded at some random party in Big Mesa, with no real friends and no ride. They'd had to call Cherie's mother to come pick them up in the Reese family minivan. Totally humiliating.

And it was all because Will wanted to help Jessica Wakefield. It was always about Jessica. Melissa suddenly felt sick to her stomach. She rolled onto her side and stared at the framed picture of Will on her nightstand.

I didn't do anything, she told herself. *So what if Cherie and Gina were picking on Jessica? Who cares? And besides, I didn't say a word.*

"What am I supposed to do? Am *I* supposed to call *you?*" she muttered to Will's sophomore-year photo. She could just imagine the conversation—or nonconversation. If she called him, they would both sit there silent, waiting for the other to apologize. Well, Will could wait forever because Melissa didn't have anything to apologize for.

"Ring," Melissa said, focusing her attention on the phone. "Come on, ring."

It rang.

Melissa grabbed the receiver. "Will?"

"No, honey. Just me." Her father's voice.

Another line picked up. "I got it, Melissa," her mother said.

"Oh, okay." Melissa dropped the phone noisily into its cradle. It was too late anyway. It was after ten. Will would already be out jogging—getting warmed up for that afternoon's game. If he hadn't called by now, he wasn't going to.

There was a loud rap at her door, and then it swung open and her mother sailed in. Melissa sometimes wondered why the woman ever bothered to knock.

"Melissa, your father was calling from Los Angeles. He should be back by . . ." Mrs. Fox stopped in the middle of the room and looked Melissa up and down. "Are you still in bed?"

"No, Mom, it just looks like I am," Melissa said.

"Nice attitude, young lady," Mrs. Fox retorted, hands on hips. Her brown hair was already pulled back in a perfect twist, and she was wearing her standard Saturday uniform—perfectly pressed chinos, a pastel plaid shirt, and pearls. Her mother crossed the room and snapped open the blinds. Melissa squinted against the sunlight. Why wasn't it raining? Her mood would go much better with rain.

"Thanks," Melissa said dryly.

Her mother started chattering on about her father and freeway traffic and something about tickets to the LA Philharmonic. But Melissa wasn't interested. Her mind was still fixated on Will and who should call whom.

"How do you live like this, Melissa?" her mother asked. She scurried around the room, picking up clothes and books and sorting everything into neat piles.

Melissa wanted to be able to ask her mom how to make everything okay with Will, but she couldn't do that. If she told her parents she was afraid of losing her boyfriend, her father would probably say something like, "Everything happens for a reason," and her mom would definitely start freaking out, criticizing Melissa for doing everything wrong and jeopardizing her relationship with Will.

Melissa scrunched down in her bed, pulling the covers back up to her chin. Will was the person Melissa always went to in a crisis. Unfortunately now Will *was* the crisis.

"Was last night fun?" Mrs. Fox asked, totally oblivious to Melissa's go-away vibe.

"Uh-huh," Melissa mumbled. *Actually, Mom, it sucked royally. I think I might have lost the only person I care about, but thanks for cleaning up my room. You've totally improved my life.*

"Did you wear the top I picked out for you?" her mother asked. She snatched up a shirt from the floor and tossed it in Melissa's hamper.

"Huh?"

Why did Jessica Wakefield have to pick that party

20

to go to last night? And if she had to be there, why couldn't she have had toilet paper hanging out of her shoe or something?

"The top I picked up for you at the mall?" Mrs. Fox prodded. She sounded kind of peeved.

Melissa blinked a few times, trying in vain to focus on what her mother was saying.

Since when does Jessica have a social life anyway?

"Honestly, Melissa." Her mother sniffed, picking up the wicker hamper with both hands. "I don't know why I bother."

"Sorry, Mom," Melissa said.

"I'm sure you are," her mother said sarcastically. She stood in the doorway, one hand on the doorknob. "I picked up bagels for breakfast. If you don't get up now, you'll have to toast your own."

"Mom, I'm a senior in high school. I know how to use a toaster," Melissa said, curling up on her side and willing her mom to disappear.

"I've had just about enough of your tone," her mother spat.

Melissa squeezed her eyes shut. "Sorry, Mom."

"You're always 'sorry' this and 'sorry' that, Melissa. Someday you're going to wish you had been nicer to your mother." And with that, her mother swept from the room, closing the door behind her.

"Could you sound any more like a movie of the week?" Melissa muttered. She didn't know whether to scream or cry. She flopped over onto her back and covered her eyes with her hands. "Please call, Will. Please. I can't take this."

But Melissa knew that the day was only going to get worse. She had a game to go to. She was going to have to pull herself out of bed, take a shower, slip into that red-and-white polyester uniform, and go act happy and hyper in front of hundreds of people.

"And I *so* feel like cheering," Melissa muttered, pulling the covers over her head. "I so feel like cheering for Will."

Once Jessica was dressed, she listened at her door to make sure no one was moving around in the hallway. If she knew Melissa Fox and her friends at all, one of them had already called Lila and told her all about last night's scene at Trent's party. The last thing Jessica needed was to be mocked to her face by her ex–best friend over breakfast.

Perfect silence.

Carrying her clogs in her hands, Jessica quietly slipped into the hallway and shut her door without a sound. Then she rushed on tiptoe down the long, thickly carpeted corridor. Jessica was getting used to this. Avoiding Lila had become second nature.

At the foot of the stairs Jessica caught a glimpse of herself in the gilded mirror on the opposite wall. She was wearing a T-shirt and black jeans. She looked fine, but it was game day. Game day without her cheerleading uniform. Jessica ignored the little pang in her chest and turned away from her reflection. It was only one game. There were still ten more to go.

"I can't believe Laufeld's making me go to pregame practice," Jessica muttered as she made her way to the kitchen. It was going to be so embarrassing to have to just sit there and watch. The coach had told her that she was still a member of the team and it was her responsibility to be there. It would promote "team unity." What a joke. The Sweet Valley High varsity cheerleading squad couldn't be more divided.

Jessica pushed open the swinging door to the kitchen just as the phone rang. She froze. Eduardo got up from the kitchen table and answered it.

"Hold one moment, please," Eduardo said.

"Is that for me?" Jessica asked. *Jeremy. Please be Jeremy.*

"No, Miss Jessica," Eduardo said. "It is for Miss Lila." He pushed a button to buzz Lila's room and hung up.

Jessica grimaced. "Of course."

Eduardo gathered up his newspaper and tucked it under his arm. "Mrs. Pervis has the morning off," he said. "Is there anything I can get for you, Miss Jessica?"

"No, thanks, Eddie," she said, earning a sour glance from the butler. "I can find my way around."

"Very well, miss," Eduardo said. He turned and pushed through the far door.

Sighing, Jessica trudged over to the huge refrigerator and yanked it open. It was stocked to overflowing with every food known to man. Unfortunately Jessica was no longer very hungry. How could Jeremy have just stood there and not come after her? How could she have misjudged him so thoroughly? It was eating her up inside.

Jessica glanced at the phone on the wall.

She *had* to know.

"Enough of this 'poor me' stuff," Jessica said, slamming the refrigerator door.

She walked across the room and pushed the button to connect with a new line. Mr. Fowler had five separate phone lines running through the house for all his important business calls. Over the years Lila had managed to appropriate three of them.

Jessica quickly dialed Jeremy's number before she could chicken out. As the phone started to ring, she realized she had no idea what she was going to say. Should she act like he'd done nothing wrong and apologize for running out? Should she launch into an explanation of Cherie and Gina's bitchiness? Should she accuse him of being a totally ignorant waste of space?

Her finger hovered nervously over the off button on the sleek handset. Four rings, five rings, six—

The line clicked. Jessica's heart leaped into her

throat as her courage fell to her feet. Then the un-mistakable sound of an answering machine filled her ears. "Thanks for calling. You've reached 555-7371. Please leave us a message and—"

Jessica panicked. She couldn't say what she needed to say to a machine. And what if he was screening his calls?

"No way," Jessica said, pressing the off button. She wasn't going to babble onto a tape while he was sitting there listening.

The door swung open, and Lila came sauntering into the room, humming happily. Jessica froze, hoping Lila wouldn't see her standing there clutching the phone like an idiot. She watched silently as Lila opened the fridge and pulled out a small bottle of orange juice. Then she spun around, pleated skirt twirling, and looked right at Jessica.

Jessica's heart skipped a beat. "Lila," she said flatly, steeling herself for a mock fest.

Lila's eyes flicked over Jessica's outfit. "Jessica," she said. Then she turned and flounced out of the room. It was the most civil interaction they'd had in weeks.

Jessica let out a breath. "I have to call Liz."

She turned on the phone again and dialed the Sandborns' number. "Please be there," she whispered, crossing her fingers.

"Hello?"

"Hi, Megan," Jessica said, recognizing Conner's sister's voice. "It's Jessica. Is Liz there?"

"I think so. Hold on a sec. Liz!" Megan screamed. Jessica held the phone away from her ear. "It's your sister!"

Jessica heard footsteps in the background and then another extension picked up.

"Hey, Jess," Elizabeth said, sounding out of breath. "What's up?"

"Nothing. Absolutely nothing is up," Jessica said, leaning against the wall. "Everything is completely down."

"This doesn't sound good," Elizabeth said.

"It's not. I have to sit out the game today, remember?" Jessica said. "And Liz, you would never believe what happened to me last night—"

"Wait, Jess. Hold that thought," Elizabeth said. "Maria's going to be here any second to pick me up. Can we talk about this later?"

Jessica's face fell. "But I *really* need to talk to you," she said, suddenly near tears. Why was everyone abandoning her lately?

"Why don't I come to the game and sit with you?" Elizabeth suggested. "You can tell me everything then."

"Really?" Jessica asked. "Liz, I would *so* appreciate it."

"Okay, Maria and I are going to brunch now, so I might be a little late, but I'll be there," Elizabeth said.

"Thanks, Liz," Jessica said, her spirits lifting slightly. "I'll be near the back of the bleachers."

Jessica was smiling as she returned the phone to

its cradle. She couldn't wait to unload on Elizabeth. It was always the best remedy.

Conner McDermott jogged into his driveway and bent over at the waist, gasping for breath. He placed his hands on his knees for support.

"What's wrong with me?" Conner said between breaths. "I didn't even run a mile." He stood up and tipped back his head, letting the morning sun warm his face as his pulse began to slow. He'd totally slacked off on running this summer. And he'd only gone out that morning because he couldn't stand being in the house, wondering when Elizabeth was going to get up. But as he leaned down to do a few quick stretches, he was glad he'd gone. At least now he knew how much work he was going to have to do before next spring's track season.

If I even decide to run again this year, Conner thought. He'd only been badgered into running last year when the phys-ed teacher had told him it was join the team or flunk gym. Apparently he'd skipped too many classes, but on the days when he *had* shown up, he'd made the mistake of running well.

Conner took one deep breath and let it out slowly, feeling his muscles relax. When he'd woken up this morning, every fiber of his being was tense. Now he felt purged. Ready to face anything. Ready to deal with Elizabeth.

He caught a glimpse of his reflection in the front

window and grimaced. His short hair was plastered to his forehead, and his face was all red. Maybe he'd deal with Elizabeth after a shower.

Just then the front door was flung open and Elizabeth walked out onto the steps. Conner's already pounding heart skipped a few beats. She was rummaging through her bag, so she hadn't seen him yet. It gave Conner a chance to regain his composure. Not that the sun in her golden hair and the short length of her denim shorts rattled him. Not at all.

"Hey," Conner said, running a hand over his saturated hair.

Elizabeth looked up, obviously startled. "Hi," she said with a wide smile. One of those flirty smiles the wearer couldn't control. One that mirrored Conner's own.

He quickly wiped his face on the sleeve of his T-shirt and tried to think of something to say. Something that wouldn't make him sound too eager. "Going somewhere?" he asked. *That was brilliant.*

Elizabeth's smile wavered slightly, and her gaze darted to the road behind him. "Um, yeah," she said, pulling the door closed and walking tentatively toward him. "To get something to eat. I'm waiting for a ride."

"Oh," Conner said, stunned to realize he was disappointed she was going out.

"So, you look like you could use a shower," Elizabeth said.

28

"Thanks a lot," Conner said, causing Elizabeth's face to ripen.

"I just meant . . . I thought you might want to get inside," Elizabeth stammered. "I mean, get out of the sun."

She was so annoyingly cute when she was flustered. Conner took a step toward her and watched as she fought to stand her ground. "I'm sorry," he said. "Do I stink or something?"

Elizabeth gazed at him, a teasing glint in her mesmerizing blue-green eyes. She sniffed and shrugged one shoulder. "Only slightly."

"Slightly's not bad," Conner said. He ran a finger down Elizabeth's bare arm and smirked as she shivered.

But then she quickly stepped aside and placed her hand over her forearm where his finger had been. "Conner, I really think you should go inside," she said.

Conner's stomach turned. He took a step back and studied her almost frightened expression. "Why are you trying to get rid of me?" he asked, narrowing his eyes.

At that moment Conner heard a car pull to a stop on the street behind him. Elizabeth blanched, and Conner turned around to see what had her so freaked. It was Maria. Conner felt the color drain from his own face. This was one scenario he did not want to deal with.

Maria glanced out the side window, and an expression of total hatred slid over her face. She turned forward and gripped the steering wheel as if she were squeezing the life out of it.

Conner looked at Elizabeth. "I think I'll go inside."

"Good idea," Elizabeth said.

Conner felt that he should say something in parting, like, "I'll see you later," or, "When will you be back?" But Elizabeth was already jogging across the yard to Maria's car. Elizabeth was definitely going to get an earful about what a hateful person Conner was. The pitfalls of hooking up with two best friends. At least *he* didn't have to deal with Maria. Conner briefly wondered if Elizabeth would tell Maria about what was going on between the two of them, but then pushed the thought aside. It wasn't his problem.

Conner sighed and walked into the blessedly air-conditioned foyer. When the cold air hit him, he felt like his senses had just cleared.

"When will you be back?" he mocked himself. "Thank *God*, you didn't say that." As he took the stairs to his room two at a time, Conner laughed at his near slipup. The last thing he needed was for Elizabeth to think he was looking forward to seeing her. So what if he'd been up all night, anticipating their next kiss?

She definitely didn't need to know that.

TIA RAMIREZ

To: marsden1@swiftnet.com
cc: mcdermott@cal.rr.com, lizw@cal.rr.com,
  mslater@swiftnet.com, jess1@cal.rr.com
From: tee@swiftnet.com
Time: 11:15 A.M.
Subject: tonight, the riot!

hey, guys!
  tonight, nine-thirty, stress-relief
time at the riot. i'll tell angel.
adios, and i better see you there! right
now i'm off to cheer like a maniac.
  GO, GLADIATORS!
                              —tia

Jeremy Aames

<u>Things</u> <u>to</u> <u>Do</u>:

Call Coach Anderson and tell him I have a family emergency and won't make today's game.

Call Trent and tell him about Dad so he's not surprised when Anderson grills him on the subject.

Pick up stuff for Dad from home:
—Walkman so he can listen to the
    San Diego game tomorrow
—robe
—slippers
—cookie-dough ice cream (if he's allowed)

Also bring back history and physics books for me.

Stop in and see Emma and Trisha.

Call Ally and give her above excuse for tomorrow morning's shift. (No need to make up two different excuses.)

Make Mom go home and get some rest.

Call Jessica.

CHAPTER

Elizabeth settled back in her seat and tried to relax as Maria made the turn off Myrtle Avenue. The tension in the car was smothering her as the nerve-racked pounding of her heart drowned out all other sounds.

There's nothing to worry about. Maria doesn't know anything. She's just mad at Conner, Elizabeth told herself. Unfortunately none of her rationalizations made her feel any less guilty about kissing Conner.

"Thanks for being ready," Maria said quietly, slipping her dark sunglasses over her eyes.

Elizabeth had been so involved in her own thoughts that Maria's soft voice made her jump. "Um, sure," she said, forcing a smile.

More silence.

Elizabeth cleared her throat. "Nice hat," she said.

Maria came to a stop at a light. She touched her floppy fisherman's cap, adjusting it slightly. "Thanks. It hides my raging zit."

"I really don't see it," Elizabeth assured her.

"That's because it's hidden."

"Oh." *Duh.*

More silence. Maria had yet to look at Elizabeth. Was she upset just because Elizabeth had been talking to Conner, or could she read the treachery all over Elizabeth's face? Elizabeth swallowed hard and took a long, deep breath. Handling paranoia was never her strong suit.

Maria popped a tape into the dashboard stereo as the light turned green. An upbeat hip-hop tune flooded the car at a low volume. Elizabeth couldn't help noticing how off mood the music was, but at least it broke the stillness.

"So, what's new?" Elizabeth asked. *Good line, Liz. Very Brady.*

"Not much," Maria said.

"Yeah. Me neither," Elizabeth replied, wondering when she'd become illiterate.

"Actually," Maria said suddenly, "there is something I wanted to talk to you about."

"Yeah?" Elizabeth prompted.

"It's about Conner."

Uh-oh. Elizabeth gripped her sweaty hands together in her lap. Could Maria possibly know what was going on? "Yeah, that was pretty awkward back there in front of his house," Elizabeth said slowly, trying to keep it vague.

"That's not it," Maria said. "Just seeing him doesn't really get to me anymore. I mean, last week we had some pretty normal conversations. There's something else." Maria paused as she pulled the car into the parking lot outside the Eggshell. She snagged a space and killed the engine but kept staring through the windshield. "This isn't easy, Liz," she said, pulling off her sunglasses and slipping them into her purse.

Elizabeth went into full panic mode. Maria knew. There was no other explanation for her doomsday tone. *I am a horrible friend*, Elizabeth thought.

"Maria—," Elizabeth started.

"Please, Liz. Just let me get this out," Maria interrupted, glancing at Elizabeth out of the corner of her eye. She unbuckled her seat belt, turned in her seat to face her friend, and took a deep breath. "I saw the poem."

Elizabeth felt all the blood rush from her face, leaving her light-headed. "You saw—" She stopped and licked her lips. This was not a good time to lose it.

"The poem. The one in your creative-writing notebook?" Maria prodded. "The love poem with Conner's name written all over the margins."

Oh. My. God.

"How did you—"

"I wasn't snooping, Liz, I swear," Maria said, growing more animated by the second. It was as if Elizabeth's composure was being sucked right out of her and pumped into Maria. "But the other day at lunch I went into your bag to get the English assignment, and I pulled out the wrong notebook."

"And you saw the rough draft of my poem," Elizabeth said. Okay, there had to be a way to explain this.

"Yeah. It was about Conner, wasn't it?" Maria asked point-blank. "Elizabeth, do you like him or something?"

Elizabeth looked into Maria's vulnerable brown eyes, her brows raised in question . . . and laughed. The sound of her laughter surprised her, but she couldn't stop.

"This isn't funny, Liz," Maria said, bringing Elizabeth up short.

"*Me?* Like *Conner?*" Elizabeth said. "Sounds pretty funny to me." *What am I saying?* Elizabeth wondered. *Just tell her the truth!* But telling the truth would destroy Maria, and Elizabeth couldn't bring herself to do it. Somewhere in the back of her totally irrational mind, she felt there had to be some other answer—some other way to get them all through this soap-opera situation unscathed. She just needed some more time to figure it all out.

"So you don't like him," Maria said, looking half relieved, half skeptical.

"No," Elizabeth said, somehow managing to look her friend in the eye.

"Then what was that poem all about?" Maria asked.

Good question. "Well . . . I was trying to write the poem for creative-writing class, and I'd been working on it all week. It was the night before it was due, and I still had nothing," Elizabeth said. So far, no lies. "So I sat down all ready to concentrate, and two seconds later Conner decides to play Conner the rock star in the next room."

Maria raised an eyebrow and smirked. Elizabeth knew she was amused by the idea of Conner playacting. It made her stomach turn, but she plunged ahead.

"So this horrible, loud guitar music comes blaring through my wall, and I can't even form a phrase, so I kept writing his name in the margins because I was so frustrated with him." If Maria bought that, it would be a miracle. "Did you notice the kind of jagged, angry scrawl? I never write like that."

"I guess." Maria leaned back against the car door, her face lined with doubt. "But why didn't you just go tell him to shut up?"

"I tried," Elizabeth said quickly. "Megan and I both pounded on his door, but he couldn't hear us. Or he just pretended not to hear us. He's so selfish, it's not even funny." Elizabeth couldn't even look Maria in the face. She stared out at the parking lot as if she was trying to get over Conner's arrogance, but she was really trying to figure out when she'd become such a smooth liar. She felt like hurling.

"Really?" Maria asked.

Elizabeth hesitated, lowering her lashes. "Yeah," she said quietly.

"Ookay," Maria said slowly. "But then who were you writing that poem about?"

Elizabeth shrugged. "I don't know. No one, really. Maybe just the guy I'm hoping I'll meet one day, you know? The guy who will eventually sweep me off my feet."

"Sappy enough?" Maria said with a laugh. "You're such a hopeless romantic."

Elizabeth glanced at Maria. She was out of the woods. Maria was buying it. But it didn't matter because Elizabeth still felt like the scum of the earth.

"I'm really sorry, Liz," Maria said. "I'm always jumping to the most unlikely conclusions. I know you guys, like, hate each other."

Swallowing back the bile caused by her deep personal disgust, Elizabeth tried to smile. "It's no big deal," she said. *I can't believe I'm letting Maria apologize to me.* "But Maria, we don't really *hate* each other anymore. I mean, living in the same house . . . It just seems like getting along makes life easier." There. First let Maria adjust to Elizabeth and Conner's friendship, and the rest could come later.

"That's very mature of you, Liz," Maria said. "You don't have to apologize for making your living situation more . . . livable."

"Thanks," Elizabeth said.

"So, brunch?" Maria asked, popping open the driver's-side door.

"Sounds good!" Elizabeth answered, trying to match Maria's new, bright tone. *Now I just have to figure out how I'm going to get any food down.*

Melissa trudged down the stairs in her cheerleading uniform, feeling only slightly better after a long, hot shower. The one good thing about having a game that afternoon was the inevitability factor. She and Will both had to be there, and there was no way he could avoid her. Of course, Melissa still hadn't figured out exactly what she was going to say when she saw him. She just knew she had to confront him before all the thinking drove her crazy.

At the bottom of the steps she turned the corner and froze, her hand still gripping the banister. Will was hunched over at the breakfast table, rubbing his eyes. His blond hair was slightly greasy, and he'd thrown on a pair of jeans and a wrinkled T-shirt. But even totally disheveled, he'd never looked so good to Melissa.

He was up all night too, Melissa realized, her worried heart soaring. *He's just as upset as I am.*

Will hadn't seen her yet, and Melissa took a moment to adopt an outward calm. She couldn't show him how excited and relieved she was to see him. He'd ditched her, and he owed her an apology.

Melissa wasn't going to give an inch until she got what she deserved.

"Will?" she said, striding into the kitchen.

He slowly pulled his hands away from his face and crossed his arms on the table in front of him. "Melissa," he said coolly.

Melissa's spirit instantly plummeted along with her conviction. Will never used her full first name, and he never took this detached tone with her. Suddenly she didn't need that apology—not even a stupid little "am-I-off-the-hook-yet?" shrug. She just wanted him to call her "Liss."

"How long have you been here?" Melissa asked, standing across the table from him and placing her hands on the back of a chair. "Why didn't you come up to my room?"

"You were in the shower," he said wearily. His beautiful gray-blue eyes were dark and clouded beneath their thick lashes. "We need to talk, okay?"

"Okay," she said slowly, a cold feeling of dread washing over her.

"Why don't you sit down?" Will suggested.

"I'm fine," Melissa replied, gripping the chair as if it was her only link to sanity.

"Fine." Will heaved a sigh and clasped his hands together. "I'm not comfortable, Liss."

"Not comfortable," Melissa repeated. What was that supposed to mean?

"Um, I haven't been comfortable for a while." His

eyes darted from the floral centerpiece on the table, to the wall, to the floor and back again. Anywhere but at Melissa. "I . . . man, this is so hard to say."

Then don't say it, Melissa begged silently.

"Okay, here it is." He took a deep breath. Melissa held hers. "I want to break up."

Melissa's stomach contracted as if she'd just been slammed in the gut by a pro boxer.

Will granted her a nervous glance, and Melissa just stared back. There was nothing else she could do.

"Well, I don't *want* to break up," he continued, "but I think we should."

Melissa opened her mouth to protest, but no sound came out. Her tongue felt like it was loaded down with sand.

"I need some space," Will said.

Oh, please. Not the I-need-space excuse. I deserve more than that.

"The whole changing-schools thing has really, I don't know. . . ." Did he think she was stupid? This was definitely not about changing schools. This was about Jessica Wakefield.

He looked up at her, obviously waiting for some kind of response, then exhaled impatiently. "You're not helping here," he said.

She raised her eyebrows. "I'm supposed to *help* you break up with me?" she asked, her voice low and scratchy. "That's rich."

"No. But don't you have anything to say?" Will

asked. He gripped the edge of the table, his knuckles turning white.

"Yes, I do," Melissa answered, her stomach twisting dangerously. "You need me, Will. We need each other. You can't actually be doing this. You can't actually know what this means."

He just held her gaze, steady and strong. He knew. Will was ready to move on without her.

"You're not going to be able to handle this, Will. You'll miss me—you know you will," Melissa said, her voice surprisingly calm. *I'm the one who's not going to be able to handle this. I already can't handle this.*

"I already do miss you, Liss." Will's voice was so morose, it made tears spring to Melissa's eyes. He released his strong hold on the table and rubbed his temples with his fingertips. "You've changed so much in the past few weeks. I don't even know who you are." He paused and looked down at the table, a shock of blond hair falling across his forehead. "I don't know who *I* am when we're together."

Melissa felt the blood start to rush to her face. "Don't try to make this all deep, Will. It's insulting," she said.

"Insulting?" he repeated, his eyes flashing as he lifted his chin.

"This isn't about you and your identity crisis or me being different," Melissa said. "This is about Jessica Wakefield."

Will stood up, his chair scratching against the tile floor. "Can't you get over that for five seconds?" he demanded, his teeth clenched. "I'm trying to talk about *us* here. You and me. Jessica has nothing to do with this."

Melissa covered her mouth with her hand and concentrated on not throwing up. She couldn't remember the last time Will confronted her like this. In fact, she was pretty sure he'd never confronted her like this.

"You can't tell me you've been happy with the way things have been lately," Will said, lowering his voice and taking a step toward her.

Melissa stepped back, breathing slowly through her nose in an attempt to calm down. "I haven't been happy . . . since you cheated on me," Melissa said slowly. Will took a deep breath and drew himself up straight. "Since *you* cheated on *me*, Will."

"I know, Liss," Will said. "I—"

"And this is how you make it up to me," Melissa said, a single tear spilling onto her cheek. She wiped it away quickly. Crying would have to wait. If she lost her grip in front of him, she would never get it back. "I want you to leave now."

"Come on, Melissa. Don't do this." He reached out to touch her arm, but she yanked it away.

"I don't want it to end like this," Will said slowly.

Melissa looked into his eyes and saw that the pain in them was real. He wasn't toying with her or being manipulative. He did still care.

But it didn't matter because he wanted to leave her.

"You don't really have a choice, do you, Will?" she said, her voice miraculously strong.

"Fine, then," Will said, clearly defeated. "Fine. I tried."

Don't leave, she screamed silently. "Fine," she said.

Will walked past her and out the kitchen door. Melissa crossed her arms over her chest and clung to the sleeves of her sweater for dear life. When she heard the front door close, she flinched. For the moment it was the only move she could make.

Jeremy passed the ICU desk as he was heading back to his father's room with yet more coffee. His shirt was totally wrinkled and untucked, he had a big coffee stain on his jeans, and his normally smooth, cropped hair was sticking up all over the place. He knew he looked like he'd been hit by a truck, and yet the nurse who had welcomed him last night smiled at him warmly.

"Your father is awake, Jeremy," she said.

"He is?" Jeremy asked, his tired voice cracking.

"Yep. His vitals are good. You can go talk with him if you'd like."

"That would be great. Thanks." Jeremy blew past her into the brightly lit room. His mom was sitting on the far side of the bed, speaking softly into his father's ear.

Jeremy stopped short. He had no idea what to say. How are you feeling? Sorry you almost died? Did they give you any Jell-O yet?

"Hi, Dad."

His parents looked over at him, and Jeremy's brow creased in concern. His mother had huge bags under her eyes and had lost all the color from her cheeks. His father immediately struggled to pull himself up straighter in his bed, but his thin arms were shaking as he did so. They were his parents. They weren't supposed to look this frail.

"You look better, Dad," Jeremy semi-lied. At least his father's eyes were open. That was an improvement.

Mr. Aames managed to pull off a wry half smile. "*This* is better? That's a little scary."

Jeremy smiled, relieved to hear humor in his father's voice. In the months just before his heart attack his father seemed to have very nearly lost his sense of humor. Jeremy crossed the room to his father's bedside. "Well, you definitely look better than you did last night."

"Better than dead?" Mr. Aames joked weakly.

"Howard!" Mrs. Aames admonished.

"Yeah, Dad," Jeremy said, still smiling. "Better than dead."

"Don't you have a game today?" Mr. Aames asked. "Shouldn't you be getting ready?"

Jeremy almost laughed. Just the thought of putting his football pads on made him want to collapse.

"You in a hurry to get rid of me, Dad?" he asked.

Mr. Aames smiled. "North Beach has a good defensive line. Big Mesa's gonna need your speed."

"Maybe, but I'm not going to go. I want to stay here with you."

His father's eyes flashed, taking Jeremy by surprise. The man didn't even seem to have enough strength for a defiant glance.

"What do you mean, you're not going to go?" Mr. Aames said. "Because of me? That's ridiculous."

"But Dad, I've been here all night. I've barely slept—"

"Toughen up, son," Mr. Aames said hoarsely. "Your team needs you. You haven't worked this hard for nothing. I want you to go."

Jeremy's heart twisted in his chest. He couldn't believe his father was so adamant about this. He was acting like nothing had happened. Didn't he get the fact that life-altering emergencies were just a little more important than football?

"Dad—"

"Jeremy!" It was almost a yell. Mr. Aames pressed his head back into the pillow and weakly asked Mrs. Aames for water. Jeremy glanced at his mother worriedly, and his mom shot back a pleading look as she poured out some water from a plastic pitcher.

"All right. I'll go," Jeremy said. "I was thinking about it anyway, but I wanted to wait until you woke up." Jeremy reached over his father's limp body to hand his mother her coffee.

"Thanks, honey," she said, smiling up at him, obviously grateful for his little white lie.

Jeremy's father sipped his water and shakily handed the glass back to Mrs. Aames. "Run for a hundred yards for your old man, hey?" he said.

Jeremy smiled wanly, which took some serious effort. "What am I, a Hall of Famer all of a sudden?" he said, sounding stiff even to his own ears.

"Get me a couple of touchdowns too," his father joked.

"Sure, Dad," Jeremy said. "I'll see what I can do."

Jeremy's mother followed him out of the room. Together they leaned against the wall and stared across the hall, lost for a moment in thought.

"You know I'm not going to the game," Jeremy said finally.

"I know. There's no way you could play after the night you had," Mrs. Aames responded. "But that was good of you to tell him you would play."

"I know, Mom, but now I have to leave," Jeremy said. "I wanted to stay here in case anything happened."

"If anything happens, I'll be here," his mother reminded him.

"Yeah, but when are you going to get some

sleep?" Jeremy asked. "No offense, Mom, but you look worse than he does."

Mrs. Aames cracked a smile. "Don't worry about me, Jeremy. It makes your father happy to think you're playing in that game today. That's all that matters."

Jeremy's frustration mounted. "Because having me around would do nothing for his spirits," he muttered sarcastically.

"What did you say?" Mrs. Aames asked. Jeremy took one look at her weary face and bit back his roiling emotions. He was probably just overtired, and he wasn't going to take it out on his mother.

He took a deep breath and let it out slowly. "Dad's gonna find out I didn't play," Jeremy said. "You know he's going to ask for the paper first thing in the morning."

"I'll explain it then," Mrs. Aames said. "He'll understand. I just didn't want him to get all worked up this morning. Are you going to go curl up in bed?"

"I think I'll hang out with the girls for a while," Jeremy said. "Emma must be freaking."

Mrs. Aames sighed. "That would be great. I explained everything to her on the phone, but she'll feel better if you're there. Trisha, of course, has no idea what's going on. She thinks she's at a perpetual slumber party."

"Must be nice to be six." Jeremy pushed himself away from the wall. The simple motion took a little too much effort. "Okay, I'll see you later. Try to get some rest." He leaned over and pecked his mom on the cheek. She squeezed his arm and smiled.

"You too," she said.

Jeremy turned on his heel and walked slowly down the hall. As he made his way through the mazes of hallways and swinging doors, he tried to put his disloyal thoughts behind him. His father just wanted him to play today because he wanted what was best for his son. And he probably couldn't stand the thought of Jeremy seeing him all laid up and weak. But as easy as it was to rationalize, Jeremy couldn't quash the concern that even this heart attack wasn't going to change things. His father needed him now more than ever, and he was still pushing Jeremy away.

Maria Slater

To: kenQB@swiftnet.com
From: mslater@swiftnet.com
Subject: re: Liz & (not) Conner

Hey, Ken—
   I talked to her, and she explained
all. I blew everything out of propor-
tion. (Big shock.) I can't keep her
from talking to him. I mean, they <u>are</u>
living together. I guess I'm just
jealous that they get to have a func-
tional relationship while I can barely
have a two-second conversation with
the guy.
   Oh, well. I just have to remember
the slight headway I made last week.
He did drive me over to Andy's when I
got a flat tire, and he was totally
civil to me. Right now, I just want to
stop thinking about it. I feel like
I'm one paranoia short of obsessed.
Maybe dancing tonight will help me re-
lease some tension.
   Speaking of which, do you want to
come out tonight? We're all going to
the Riot at nine-thirty. You should
show.
                         WB,
                         Maria

Ken Matthews

To: mslater@swiftnet.com
From: kenQB@swiftnet.com
Subject: tonight

Maria—
   Cool. I knew you guys would work it
out. And you sound much better. I'll
have to pass on tonight, though. Not
exactly the dancing type. But thanks
for asking.

                                —Ken

CHAPTER
A Lost Cause
4

Melissa was not going to cry. There was no use crying over something that wasn't really happening, and this breakup wasn't really happening. She wouldn't let it.

Taking a deep breath, Melissa squared her shoulders and walked across the kitchen. She ignored the shaking in her legs and the pounding of her heart. She had to act like nothing was wrong. If she faked it, she had a better chance of making it true.

Coffee. She just needed some coffee and some time alone to figure out what to do next. She removed a mug from the cabinet and placed it on the counter. That was when she noticed she'd chosen the mug Will had given her in junior high for Valentine's Day. It had little hearts all over it, and it had once been filled with chocolate kisses and heart candies.

"I can't believe you broke up with me," Melissa said, her voice sounding empty and distant. He had promised her that he would always be there, always be with her, always be her Will. This had to be a bad dream. It was a continuation of last night's nightmare.

"It helps to actually put the coffee in the cup, Melissa." Her mother's voice suddenly invaded her thoughts. Mrs. Fox's shoes clicked as she strode across the kitchen.

Melissa closed her eyes tightly against a sudden wave of tears. *Not now. Please go away, Mom. Please don't talk to me.*

"I was still deciding whether or not to have coffee," Melissa said evenly.

"Well, I need to clean the pot, so decide now."

Melissa automatically held out her cup, which her mother filled. Then she just placed the cup back in front of her. Every limb felt like lead, so going for the sweetener just seemed like too much of a hassle.

Melissa's mother glanced around the room as she rinsed out the glass coffee pitcher. "Did Will leave?"

A tear spilled over, and Melissa once again wiped it away before her mother could see.

"Yeah," she said, her voice cracking. *Yes, he left. He's gone for good.*

"Melissa?" her mother said, shutting off the water and leaning her hip against the counter. She stared at the side of Melissa's face. "Are you all right?"

Melissa's heart flopped. Did her mother actually just ask her that? She glanced at her mom, ready to gush out the entire story. To just cry and let her mom tell her everything was going to be fine. But before she could say a word, her mother jumped right in.

"Because you look terrible," she said. "Are you really going to the game like that?"

Melissa looked down at her uniform and blinked back tears.

"I mean, I thought you and Will would be going together, but it's a good thing you stayed behind," Mrs. Fox continued, turning back to the sink to scrub the pot. "Why don't you go upstairs and do something with your hair?"

Reaching back shakily, Melissa touched her pony-tail. Normally she'd have a sarcastic comeback for her mother, but right now she just had to get out of the room. She was not going to cry in front of the witch. She just refused.

"Okay," she said, turning to leave.

"Either take your coffee or clean up after yourself," her mother called after her, but Melissa was already halfway up the stairs. Blinded by tears, she practically fell into her room, slamming the door behind her.

Melissa walked directly to the box of tissues on her desk and wiped her face clean. She blew her nose, took a deep breath, and pulled the band out of her hair. Then she walked over to her full-length mirror and almost fainted. She looked like death warmed over.

"I can't do this," she said. "I can't go to the game. I can't *cheer*."

She sniffled and turned away from her blotchy reflection. "How do I face Will? If I don't talk to him, everyone will ask me what's going on, and then I'll have to tell them. . . ." She paused and drew in a shaky breath. "I'll have to tell them he dumped me."

Suddenly a horrifying thought occurred to her, and her heart seemed to stop beating and turn cold. What if Will told his friends and word got around? What if everyone already knew by the time she got to the game and they were all pitying and condescending?

What if Jessica found out?

Even worse, what if Will went right to Jessica and told her?

Melissa could just imagine the smug grin on Jessica's face when she realized that Melissa was too distraught to show up. There was no way Melissa would give her the satisfaction of thinking she'd won. She smoothed down the front of her sweater and lifted her chin. Suddenly her tears had dried up and a new emotion had taken over. Defiance.

She was going to have to get through the game. After that, a bawling fit would be more than necessary.

Elizabeth sailed through the front door in a rush, glad to be free of Maria even if it was only for five seconds. Maria was waiting outside to give Elizabeth a ride to the game. Unfortunately, in her panicked rush to get out of the house that morning, Elizabeth had forgotten her wallet, and her friend had been forced to pay for brunch. Maria had driven all the way back to the Sandborns' so Elizabeth could get money for the game and pay Maria back. Now Elizabeth was running seriously late.

"See what happens when you let certain people get to you?" Elizabeth muttered. "You go brain dead."

She ran upstairs, taking the steps two at a time, grabbed her wallet from her dresser, and barreled back down. When she hit the bottom step, her stomach growled audibly—probably because her guilt had prevented her from eating more than half a croissant at brunch. Elizabeth pulled open the front door and signaled to Maria to wait one more minute.

"Take your time!" Maria yelled.

Elizabeth closed the door and ran for the kitchen.

"Love football. Love football," she muttered, trying to psych herself up. Football games had always been Jessica's thing. Elizabeth was lucky if she knew who had the ball and which end zone they were going for. "Love football," she repeated as she walked into the kitchen.

"Really, Liz? That's amazing," Conner said dryly.

Heart pounding, Elizabeth stopped and looked up. Conner was leaning against the counter at the far side of the kitchen, and Mrs. Sandborn was searching the refrigerator, tossing the contents around noisily.

"Hey," Elizabeth said. Conner nodded. "Hi, Mrs. Sandborn."

59

Conner's mother stood slowly. "Hello, Elizabeth," she said with a slight smile. "Off to the game?" She rested one arm on the top of the open refrigerator door and squinted at Elizabeth. She looked like she'd just rolled out of bed.

"Yeah, actually, I'm running late," Elizabeth said, trying hard to ignore Conner's intent stare. "Can you just hand me an orange?"

"Sure," Mrs. Sandborn said, pulling open the produce drawer. She grabbed an apple and handed it to Elizabeth.

"Mom, she said an orange," Conner said, crossing the room with one stride and taking the apple from Elizabeth's hand.

Mrs. Sandborn shrugged. "Sorry, sweetie." She blinked at Conner. "You'd think it was a capital crime."

Elizabeth smiled and held out her hand to Conner. "I'll take that. It's fine." Conner dropped the apple into Elizabeth's hand. "I'll see you guys later," Elizabeth said, turning on her heel and hurrying out of the room.

When she heard Conner's footsteps behind her, Elizabeth's heart bounced up into her throat.

"How are you getting to the game?" Conner asked. Elizabeth turned around as he stuffed his hands in the front pockets of his battered, form-fitting jeans.

"Maria's waiting outside," Elizabeth said, amazed that he even asked.

"Oh." Conner looked past Elizabeth toward the front door. "That's too bad. I would have driven you." He took a step closer, and Elizabeth felt her palms start to sweat. He reached out and brushed her jaw with the back of one finger. Elizabeth was overcome by chills as her knees weakened.

"No, Conner," Elizabeth said. "We can't."

"Can't we?" He came closer still. Elizabeth inhaled the scent of his aftershave, and her logic temporarily fogged over.

"No." She shook her head, baffled by her self-control.

Conner stopped his advance. "What's wrong?"

"I just spent the last couple of hours lying to Maria," Elizabeth said. "She's my best friend. I just can't take this." *But you can kiss me,* she thought. *You can if you really want to.*

"Forget Maria," Conner said.

"It's not that easy," Elizabeth said, staring into the depths of his beautiful green eyes. "Besides," she said, glancing away. "We're all wrong for each other anyway. It's never going to work."

There was a moment of silence, and then Conner stepped back. "Okay," he said.

Elizabeth's heart skipped a beat. *Okay?* "And with you and me living in the same house . . ." *Argue with me. Come on. Say something.*

"Right," Conner said.

Elizabeth blinked. Oh God. He really didn't care. "And Maria's my best friend."

"I think you mentioned that," Conner said with a half smile.

"Yeah? Well . . . that's because it's true," Elizabeth said, willing herself to shut up. But she couldn't. Her nerves were shot. "And besides—"

"Besides?" he said, his voice deepening a bit.

Elizabeth became very aware of her breathing. "Besides . . . ," she repeated, trying to remember the "besides."

He shifted his weight from one foot to the other and put his hands on his hips. His oatmeal-colored T-shirt stretched across his chest as he moved, and it was all Elizabeth could do not to grab him.

He raised one eyebrow.

"It's just wrong," she finished lamely.

"Fine," he said. He knitted his brow, looked at the floor as if he was thinking it over, and then repeated himself. "Fine."

Elizabeth felt her spirits slide completely off the charts. "Fine," she agreed, but her voice didn't really sound with any conviction. But this was good. This was a good thing. No more guilt, no more sneaking around. Elizabeth nodded once and turned to leave.

"Hey," Conner said.

She turned around, and Conner pulled her into his arms. Before she could breathe, he was kissing her. He reached up and placed his hands on her face as Elizabeth clung to the front of his T-shirt, completely taken off guard and completely light-headed.

They completely bypassed the typical, tender initial kiss and plunged right into an urgent, feverish, searching, grasping, tangled kiss. Elizabeth tried to pull back for air, but he wouldn't let her. *Forget Maria,* she heard his voice in her mind. Elizabeth was a lost cause.

Then, just as abruptly as he'd grabbed her, Conner pulled away. Elizabeth stumbled, her balance completely thrown. Still trying to catch her breath, she looked up at him.

Conner grinned, his eyes heavy. He looked half drunk, half triumphant.

A horn honked in the driveway, and Elizabeth almost jumped.

"I have to go," she said, frozen in place.

"So go," Conner said.

Elizabeth just stood there, unable to control a single muscle in her body.

"Have fun at the game," Conner called as he turned and headed up the stairs.

Elizabeth blinked as if she were coming out of a trance. She reached back shakily and found the doorknob with her hand even as her mind followed Conner up to his room. This was going to be the longest football game in history.

Jessica stood in the bathroom at school, waiting until the absolute last second before she went out to the field. Standing off to the side during practice had been hard enough. But sitting in the stands while everyone else cheered was going to be a nightmare.

"Oh, just get out there, Wakefield," she said to her reflection. The rest of the squad was decorating the stands with streamers and balloons. She probably wasn't forbidden from helping with that.

Jessica pasted on a smile and headed out the door and through the back exit of the gym. She was within sight of the gate leading to the playing field and spectator stands when she spotted Will.

Jessica only hesitated a split second before she regained her composure. She didn't want to give him the satisfaction of knowing he'd rattled her. But what was he doing, hanging by the fence? He was already dressed for the game—full padding, number-nine jersey, cleats, helmet looped over his forearm, black stripes under his eyes. He should have been warming up with the rest of the team.

Just my luck, Jessica thought. *The one day he decides to become undedicated, I have to bump into him.*

She tried to walk right by him, refusing to make eye contact.

"Hey, Jessica," Will said.

Damn. She had almost made it. But it stood to reason that he had called out to her. After all, her weekend had thus far sucked. Why break the streak? Jessica just kept walking.

"Wait up," Will called, jogging to catch up with her.

Jessica considered doing the whole "I-can't-hear-you"

act, but on second thought she stopped. Every time he'd tried to talk to her in the past, she'd walked away, either too upset or too scared to listen. For some reason, she just didn't feel like running today. She was sick of running. She set her jaw and calmly turned around.

"Here to pick up where your girlfriend and her friends left off last night?" she said coolly.

Will's step faltered, and he looked at the ground. "Jessica, I tried to stop them—"

"Oh, please," Jessica said. "You're so full of it." Okay, so maybe she was going to walk away. But it felt good. She backed up a step.

"I'm sorry," Will said.

"I've heard that one before," Jessica pointed out.

"Jessica—"

"Will." Her I-mean-business tone brought him up short. "How many times have I asked you to just leave me alone?"

"Jessica, calm down. I just want to—"

"I am so sick of you people!" Jessica shouted, startling even herself. She noticed a couple of bleacher-bound parents glance warily in her direction and blushed. But a few spectators couldn't deter her at this point.

"Us people?" Will asked, his brow furrowing.

"Guys!" Jessica exclaimed, throwing out her arms. She was exploding, but she didn't care. "You're so wrapped up in yourselves and your stupid sports and your stupid images. I don't even know why I bother. You don't care about anyone but yourself. None of you do."

Jessica was dimly aware that her anger should have been directed at a certain other football player from a completely different school, but she didn't care. Will deserved it too. He'd spent the whole school year so far deserving it—making her fall in love with him, lying about wanting a future with her, standing by while Melissa ruined her life, letting everyone believe that she was a total slut. Jessica's eyes stung at the memories.

"Jess, just give me a minute to explain—"

"Do you even hear what I'm saying to you?" Jessica asked, bringing her hands to her head. "I am not going to give you a minute. I'm not even going to give you a second. You're not worth my time." She stepped forward and looked him directly in the eye. She paused for only a moment when she saw the pain there. "For the last time, Will. Leave. Me. Alone."

With that Jessica spun around and walked briskly toward the bleachers. Suddenly she was feeling much, *much* better.

Elizabeth Wakefield

"Maria, I really need to talk to you about something. It's about Conner, actually. He and I—"

"Maria, you remember when we were little and you stole my Raggedy Ann doll? My favorite Raggedy Ann doll? Remember how I forgave you? Well—"

"Conner kissed <u>me</u>. . . . I swear. Every time we've kissed, he's started it. . . ." Hey, that's actually true.

Okay, okay.

"Maria, I'm in love with Conner. And there's a very slim chance he may be in love with me. Now, would you stand in the way of possible true love?"

Maybe I should take a self-defense class before I do this.

Conner McDermott

You know how when you live with somebody, you start to recognize their sounds? Like when Megan comes home, she always swings open the front door, making this loud creak, then slams it, and then she basically bounces across the foyer. When my mom comes home sober, she sort of slides into the house and efficiently strides across to the kitchen. When my mom comes home drunk, she sounds like a lumberjack or something. I swear, how a woman that skinny can have footsteps that heavy is beyond me.

But when Elizabeth comes home, you can barely hear her. Even when she's in, like, a frantic rush, she barely makes a sound. It's like she has this unconscious, inherent . . . I don't know . . . courtesy, I guess. Like she doesn't want to disturb anybody, and it's become part of her nature.

Me? I make as much noise as humanly possible.

CHAPTER 5
A Shortage of Nice Guys

"*S! V! H! S!* Let's go, Sweet Valley!"

Melissa couldn't believe the performance she was pulling off. Her smile was picture-perfect, but every time a cheer ended, the look in her eyes was just shy of hostile, nearly defiant. She wanted to make it clear that she knew everyone knew she'd been dumped—and that they'd better not mess with her. Of course, she didn't actually have the energy to back up her threatening glare.

Ever since Will's name had been announced at the beginning of the game and she'd watched him run out onto the field, Melissa had felt unbelievably tired. Her bed was miles away in El Carro, but Melissa could swear she heard it calling her name.

The red-and-white-clad crowd went wild, and Melissa threw her arms in the air and yelled along with them even though she had no clue what had just happened. Thus far, the action on the field had been one big blur. Melissa had been concentrating on the stands, trying to discern who knew and whether or not they were mocking her.

"And Simmons's pass to Wilkins is complete," the announcer shouted cheerfully. Melissa watched Will slap hands with Todd and felt like hurling.

She wanted him back. Will was her rock, her stability, her life. As Will huddled up with the rest of the offense, Tia called another cheer. Melissa got in line and smiled, even though all she wanted to do was cry and bawl and scream. She deserved an Oscar for today—and it was only the beginning of the second quarter.

What a total nightmare.

"First and ten, do it again!" she yelled in unison with the other cheerleaders. "First and ten, do it again!"

Melissa executed her moves in perfect sync with the rest of the squad. *The rest of the squad minus Jessica Wakefield,* she thought, the tiny hairs on the back of her neck standing on end. She scanned the crowd, looking for Jessica, but she was nowhere to be found.

She's probably hiding somewhere in the back, Melissa thought. *She's up there somewhere. I wonder if she knows yet. If she knows she's won.*

Will could deny it all he wanted, but Jessica had started this whole mess. She was the catalyst that had caused the breakdown of Melissa and Will's bond. And now, after everything Jessica had put Melissa through, she'd gotten exactly what she wanted. Will must have told his friends he'd dumped Melissa. He would have at least told his best friend, Josh Radinsky. Then all Josh would have to do was tell his flavor of the month, Lila Fowler, and it would be all over the stands in seconds.

Even Jessica would hear.

Lila and her friend Amy Sutton were the biggest mouths Melissa had ever encountered, and this was exactly the kind of gossip they thrived on. Melissa shot a glance at Lila. She was inspecting her nails as the guys on the field lined up for their next play. Lila hadn't said anything to Melissa, but that didn't mean much. She could have just been waiting until the game was over so she could properly focus on the details.

"Do you think Will is gonna run it in?" Gina Cho asked suddenly, flicking the end of her perfect black braid over her shoulder. Her dark eyes were shining with excitement, and she had a perky I'm-in-front-of-the-crowd smile plastered across her face. "He's playing an amazing game," she added.

Melissa paused a moment before answering. "Yeah, maybe," she said. Okay, so Gina was clueless. She was one of Melissa's best friends, and she would never have pointed out Will's attributes if she knew he'd just dumped Melissa.

"He'll have to run it," Annie Whitman said, her green eyes serious. "Pueblo Valley is sticking to Mike and Todd like superglue. It's a miracle that Todd made that last catch. And they've doubled up the defense on the running backs. Will doesn't have too many options."

Melissa raised her eyebrows. Annie should have been coaching instead of cheering. "I guess not,"

Melissa said, recognizing that it was her turn to speak. She looked at her feet and ground her toe into the newly paved, red clay track. In the stands the pep band started up the fight song, and the sound of the upbeat trumpets blaring made Melissa cringe.

"Oh, don't worry, Melissa," Gina said. "Will always finds a way to win."

"Yep. You'll be going home with the hero again," Annie said.

"Girls! Quit the chatting and get back in your lines!" Coach Laufeld called from her usual position at the foot of the packed bleachers. Melissa had to concentrate to keep from staring the compact woman down. She was such a slave driver—so much less cool than Melissa's old coach from El Carro.

But as Gina and Annie scurried back to their places, Melissa felt her expression softening into a small smile. If the squad didn't know, then maybe the situation wasn't as bad as she thought.

She focused on the game as Brian Cogley, the Sweet Valley center, got ready to hike the ball to Will.

Will had been so nervous about switching schools and having to learn to play with a new center, but Melissa had been right there by his side to help him through it. Will's old center from El Carro had been sent off to Big Mesa after the El Carro student body had been divided following the earthquake. The two of them had been playing together for years.

Will had explained his anxiety about losing his teammate by comparing the situation to his relationship with her. "We've been together so long, Liss, we can just *feel* what works." Yeah, right.

Melissa felt tears spring to her eyes and took a deep breath.

"Blue thirty-two! Blue thirty-two! Hike!" Will yelled as he surveyed the line.

Brian hiked Will the ball, and Will dropped back. He pump-faked once, then tucked the ball and dodged left. A huge linebacker was coming right at him, but Will executed a perfect spin move, ducked under the guy's arms, and ran.

"He's at the ten, the five, and . . . touchdown!" the announcer roared. "Sweet Valley quarterback Will Simmons runs it in." Confetti rained down from the stands as the crowd exploded and the band started blaring again. Melissa closed her eyes and waited for the inevitable while the shouts and cheers of the squad pierced her heart.

"Time for a Will Simmons cheer, Melissa," Gina shouted, clapping wildly.

I can't, Melissa thought. *Why couldn't you have just dropped the ball, Will?*

Every time any player scored, one of the cheerleaders got up in front of the stands and did that player's cheer. No one else ever got to do the Will Simmons cheer. That had been Melissa's territory for years.

Tia ran over to Melissa's side. "Come on, Melissa," she prodded as the rest of the squad started chanting, "Simmons! Simmons! Simmons!"

Melissa looked down briefly to clear the pain from her face. Just because the squad seemed oblivious, that didn't mean her classmates in the stands hadn't heard the news. They must have. It was too big. She and Will were the most visible couple in school. If he'd told just one person . . . Cheering with the squad was one thing, but she couldn't go out there and yell his name by herself. They would all be laughing at her, pitying her. It was so pathetic.

"Come on, Fox," Coach Laufeld yelled.

Melissa steeled herself and finally looked up at the crowd. No one was smirking. No one was laughing or shaking their heads at her. Suddenly her eyes lighted on Jessica and her sister, sitting near the back. Jessica was looking to the right, pretending to be totally enthralled by something on the bench next to her. She was purposely ignoring Melissa, not smiling triumphantly. She didn't know. No one knew.

Relief washed over Melissa as she took her position and did her cheer. She finished off with a flawless round off, back handspring, back tuck. It was her signature move, and the crowd roared their approval. Melissa grinned.

No one knew. *Thank you, Will.*

He *did* still care. And if he hadn't told anyone, there was still a chance. Maybe he was having second thoughts, so he didn't want to make the news public. Maybe he'd realized he'd made a mistake.

Melissa would find him after the game. She'd find him and make him listen. And before that night's victory party, he would be hers again.

"How are you doing?" Elizabeth asked Jessica as the teams jogged back onto the field after halftime. She placed their little cardboard box of football game food between them and grabbed up a loaded hot dog.

"Fine," Jessica lied as a cool breeze fluttered her fine, blond hair. She was much less than fine. She couldn't stop thinking about her yelling match with Will. For some strange reason, she had started to regret the fact that she hadn't let him say what he wanted to say. Will was trying to apologize to her. At least he cared enough to come after her. Unlike some people.

"You sure?" Elizabeth asked. "You're barely even here." A big glob of relish hit the wooden bleacher at their feet with a plop.

"Hungry, Liz?" Jessica asked teasingly.

Elizabeth grabbed a flimsy paper napkin with the words *Go, Gladiators* stamped across it in red ink. She chewed and swallowed before answering. "I guess that apple I had earlier didn't do it for me," she said.

"Well, you can have my hot dog too if you want it," Jessica offered. "I'm not that hungry."

"Jess, what's wrong?" Elizabeth asked in her trademark concerned tone. "You never pass up junk food."

"I'm just thinking," Jessica said, slumping slightly.

"I know watching the halftime show was hard for you, but perk up—only two quarters left," Elizabeth said, sipping her soda. "At least Laufeld let you sit with me instead of chaining you to her side."

Jessica snorted a laugh. "Believe me, the cheerleading squad is the last thing on my mind right now," she said.

"So what was it that had you so raring to talk on the phone earlier?" Elizabeth asked. "We've been here for more than an hour and you haven't even mentioned it."

Jessica sighed wearily and lowered her voice. "You know how I went out with Jeremy Aames last night?"

"Yeah," Elizabeth answered. She put down her hot dog and wiped her hands. "I asked you about it, and you said it was fine. Usually that means it was so lame, you don't want to talk about it." She pushed her hair behind her ears and studied her sister's face.

"Well, it was beyond lame," Jessica said, staring down at her hands. "It actually sucked big time." She squirmed back in her seat, sitting up straight, and looked into her sister's intent eyes. "He abandoned me to the wolves."

"I don't understand," Elizabeth said, her brow furrowing. "Wolves?"

"Yeah, a little pack called Melissa and friends," Jessica said wryly, lowering her voice. "They were in rare form last night."

Elizabeth's mouth dropped open. "But I thought the party was in Big Mesa. What were they even doing there?"

"Who knows?" Jessica said with a shrug. "Maybe they followed my scent. You know—stalking their prey." She smiled wanly.

"All right, enough with the metaphors," Elizabeth said. "What happened?"

Suddenly the spectators around Elizabeth and Jessica jumped to their feet, cheering. Elizabeth waited while Jessica stood up and peered over the heads of the guys in front of them, checking the field.

"Todd just got a first down," she said, dropping back onto the bench along with the rest of the fans.

"First down, Wilkins!" the announcer yelled. "A sixteen-yard gain on the play."

Elizabeth watched as Todd's teammates slapped him on the back and knew he was grinning somewhere under that face mask. She allowed herself a sentimental heart flop for her ex and then returned her attention to her sister. They were concentrating on Jessica's current love life, not Elizabeth's past.

"Okay, so what happened?" Elizabeth asked.

"Well, Cherie and Gina started talking about how I'd worked my way through all the male population at SVH, so I had to move on to Big Mesa," Jessica explained matter-of-factly, ducking her head slightly to keep the conversation private. "That caught everyone's attention, as you can imagine."

"Oh, Jess. I'm so sorry," Elizabeth said, touching Jessica's arm.

"So once everyone started staring and whispering and it was clear that Gina and Cherie weren't going to shut up, I just ran," Jessica finished. She vividly remembered the confused and appalled stares as she'd fled the large foyer at Trent's house. "It was so humiliating. But the point is, Jeremy didn't even come after me."

"What?" Elizabeth asked. "*Jeremy?* He's practically the sweetest guy on earth."

"Yeah, practically," Jessica scoffed. "All I know is, I waited outside at the edge of the driveway for a few minutes, you know, to give him time to come searching, and he never showed. He was probably too busy saving face in front of his friends."

"I can't believe it," Elizabeth said. "There has to be some explanation."

"That's why you're here," Jessica said, knocking her knee against Elizabeth's. "You're the rational one, so come up with an explanation. Why didn't he come after me last night?"

Elizabeth shrugged. "I don't know. Maybe he tried to find you but just missed you." Elizabeth looked out at the field as she tried to come up with an answer. "Or maybe he was busy chucking Melissa and her friends out the back door. Who knows? But I really think you should let him explain."

"Yeah, well, he hasn't even called," Jessica said.

"He will," Elizabeth assured her. "And when he does, you have to give him a chance to explain."

"I do?" Jessica asked.

Elizabeth nodded, her expression full of conviction. "You know why? Because there's a shortage of nice guys in this world. Jeremy is the first one either one of us has met in a long, *long* time."

Jessica looked out at the field as Will called out his next play. Just looking at him made her stomach turn. He'd kissed her and held her and made promises and plans. And then he'd just stood by while Melissa and her friends had ripped her apart, while they'd caused her to get suspended from the squad, and while they'd torn her down last night in front of a room full of strangers. Jessica couldn't believe she'd even thought about hearing him out.

"You're right, Liz," Jessica said. "It's been a very long time."

Melissa leaned back against the trophy case in the gym lobby and trained her eyes on the locker-room door. As soon as the final whistle had blown, she had grabbed her pom-poms and rushed to the school, determined to be there when Will was done with his postgame shower.

"I know! I couldn't believe she said that!" Lila's

voice sounded from the direction of the main hallway, followed by female laughter. Moments later Lila, Cherie, and Gina came around the corner, their cheerleading sneakers squeaking on the freshly waxed floor.

"Hey, Melissa," Lila said, tossing her hair behind her shoulders. "We're going to House of Java for a little while. Do you want to come?"

"Thanks, but I'm waiting for Will," Melissa said tentatively. She still wasn't sure who knew what.

"Of course!" Cherie said with a suggestive grin. "Will needs his kiss for a game well played."

Melissa laughed nervously. She couldn't let her uncertainty come across. Even if the conversation she was about to have went as planned, she wasn't sure Will would accept a victory kiss—yet.

"So we'll see you at Josh's house tonight, okay?" Gina asked. "Huge victory party."

"I'll be there," Melissa assured them. She casually waved good-bye as her friends headed for the parking lot. A second later the heavy, wooden locker-room door was flung open so hard, it crashed back against the cinder-block wall.

Josh Radinsky and Matt Wells barreled through, laughing and yelling as they came. In the distance Melissa could hear Will's voice echoing against the locker-room walls. She felt her face redden, but she stared directly at Will's two best friends, defying them to say anything about the breakup. She could handle these two.

"Hey! Melissa!" Matt shouted, grinning warmly. "Was that a game or what?" He ran over, picked her up with one arm grasping her waist, and spun her around. Melissa laughed as he restored her to earth.

"Nice running, Matt," Melissa said. She glanced over his broad shoulder at Josh. "And blocking, Rad," she added.

"We do what we can," Josh said with a lopsided smile. "Your man's right behind us," he went on, pushing through the glass lobby doors. "We'll see you tonight."

Melissa beamed as the guys walked down the slight grassy slope to their cars. *Your man,* Josh had said. Will hadn't even told his best friend. This could mean only one thing.

"Hey, Liss."

Liss. Melissa's heart skipped a beat at the sound of his voice. She turned slowly to find Will standing just outside the locker-room door. His blond hair was still wet and hung in saturated curls along his forehead, and his skin was still pink from the hot water.

"Nice game," Melissa said.

"Yeah." Will scratched the back of his neck as he moved away from the locker room. He didn't move toward Melissa, but just to the right. He looked up at her from his safe distance, his blue-gray eyes laced with concern. "How're you doing?"

Melissa took a step toward him. "Okay," she said.

"Yeah?" Will asked, lifting his chin.

She took another careful step closer. Will didn't move away. "Can we talk for a minute?" she asked.

"Okay," Will said. He leaned over and placed his duffel bag on the linoleum floor. "What's up?"

"I know you didn't tell anybody about what happened," Melissa said, moving within touching range. She looked up at Will through her lashes. "Does that mean what I think it means?"

"Melissa—"

She reached out and placed her hand on his chest, and Will stopped abruptly. "If you're having second thoughts, Will, I'll listen," she said quietly. "If—"

Will's hands came down softly on her shoulders. Melissa stopped breathing as he pushed her back slightly, still holding her. His touch was as gentle as it had ever been, but the action sent another message entirely.

"Melissa, look at me," Will said, gazing directly into her eyes. "I'm sorry, but I'm not having second thoughts."

"But, Will." Melissa's voice cracked, and she bit her lip. *No crying,* she reminded herself. Besides, why bother talking when she had no idea what to say?

"This is hard for me too, Melissa, but it's over." He reached up and touched her cheek. "I'm sorry. I don't know what else I can say."

Melissa took a step back, suddenly repulsed by his touch. She wrapped her arms around herself and blinked back the flood of tears that sprang to her eyes. "So why didn't you tell anyone? I mean, you didn't even tell Josh. Don't you want people to know now that you're free?" she asked bitterly. *Don't you want Jessica to know?*

The locker-room door banged open, and a stream of guys bustled through. Melissa turned her face away from them so they wouldn't see how upset she was. Will waited until they were gone to answer.

"I didn't tell anyone because I thought you'd want to tell your friends," Will said quietly, picking up his bag. "I thought I should at least let you break it to them however you wanted."

Oh. So now he was being charitable.

"I can't tell them," Melissa said. "I can't tell them you dumped me. What are they going to think?"

"So tell them *you* dumped *me*," Will said, running his free hand over his hair. "If that will make you feel better, I don't care."

Melissa stared at him through watery eyes. She knew why he was so desperate for her to talk to her friends. He was scared of what she might do if she didn't have people to support her. Scared of the blame he might face if things went . . . wrong. The way they had once before.

"Do you promise not to tell anyone until I let you know I've dealt with it?" Melissa asked.

"I won't," Will said, taking a step toward her. She backed away even farther, and Will sighed in frustration.

"But tell them soon, Melissa. They're your friends. They're going to want to listen and . . . help you."

"Uh-huh," Melissa said, barely holding back the sobs.

"I wish there was some way I could make it easier, Liss," Will said. "I really do." He waited for a response he knew he wasn't going to get, and then he turned and pushed through the glass doors.

"I know you do," Melissa said, watching his back as he moved away from her. When she heard the pathetic waver in her voice, she couldn't take it anymore. She grabbed her things and ran to the bathroom, loud sobs escaping from her throat.

Will Simmons

We won. The Sweet Valley
High Gladiators are two and oh.
Too bad I'm oh and two when it
comes to girls.

I just can't believe I played that
well today. I mean, I was up all
night trying to figure out what to
say to Melissa and playing out all
her possible reactions and my
reactions to her reactions. But I have
to say, I didn't expect her to act the
way she did. To handle it so coolly. I
expected her to freak, to throw
things, to cry and scream and
threaten.

And then that scene after the
game. The fact that she'd gotten her
hopes up and I had to just let her

down all over again. She looked so upset and so frail. It scared me. It was just all too familiar.

A tantrum would have been easier to handle. Right now, I don't know what's going through her head, and I don't like not knowing. With Melissa there are too many possibilities.

Too many really scary possibilities.

CHAPTER
Without Regret
6

Elizabeth picked up the phone on the first ring.

"Liz? It's Tia."

"Hey, Tee! Nice game. Excellent cheering going on there."

"Yeah, right. We totally flubbed on the spider pyramid, and the double-base extensions didn't exactly . . . extend," Tia said with a groan.

"Tee?"

"Yeah?"

"No idea what you're talking about right here," Elizabeth said.

Tia laughed. "Sorry. Guess I forgot which twin I had on the phone. So, listen, are you coming to the Riot tonight?"

"Definitely. I can't wait to get out of the house," Elizabeth said.

"Cool. Is Conner coming?"

That's why I want to get out of the house. "I don't know. Want me to get him?"

"Please."

"Conner! Phone!" Elizabeth yelled.

The line picked up. "Hello?" Conner said.

"Conner? It's Tia."

"Bye, guys!" Elizabeth said. She dropped the phone on the cradle. *If Conner goes, I won't go,* she told herself. *Or maybe I should go if Conner goes. Actually, it all depends on whether Maria is going. . . .*

"So, are you coming tonight, Conner?" Tia asked.

Conner sighed. "I don't know. Is Elizabeth going?"

"Yep. She sounded psyched," Tia said.

"I don't know. Maybe I will," Conner said.

"Commitmentphobe," Tia teased.

"What's that supposed to mean?" Conner demanded.

"Nothing! Just that you never want to make plans. Harsh enough?"

"Sorry," Conner muttered.

"Listen, I've got some other calls to make," Tia said. "Let me know when you decide."

She dropped the phone the second Elizabeth yelled, "Are you off?"

"Yeah!" Conner yelled back.

Elizabeth quickly dialed Maria's number.

"Maria?" Elizabeth asked.

"Hey, Liz. What's up?" She sounded chipper.

"Are you coming to the Riot tonight?" Elizabeth asked.

"Oh. I think so. I invited Ken, if you can believe it," she said.

Elizabeth's eyebrows shot up. "Ken Matthews?" she asked.

"Yeah, I know. But he's actually been very cool lately," Maria said. There was a click on the line. "Hold on a sec. I have another call," Maria said.

Does Maria like Ken? Elizabeth thought. No, it wasn't possible. Maria still liked—

"Liz?" Maria was back. "Ken's not coming. Apparently he sent me an e-mail, but I haven't checked it yet. I don't think he's up to being truly social yet."

"Oh. That was him?" Elizabeth asked.

"No, I just made that all up," Maria joked.

"Very funny. You two aren't, like, a *thing*, are you?" Elizabeth asked, realizing how much easier a thing between Ken and Maria would make her life.

"Oh, *no*," Maria said. "We've just been hanging out. I've been talking to him about . . . stuff. Anyway, is Conner coming tonight?"

The door to Elizabeth's room opened, and Elizabeth practically jumped off her bed.

"Sorry," Conner said.

"Hold on, Maria," Elizabeth said into the phone. She covered the mouthpiece with her hand. "What?" she hissed at Conner.

"Are you going tonight?" he whispered.

Elizabeth felt her cheeks turn pink. "Yeah, I think so. You?"

"Yeah, I think so." He closed the door.

Damn. Now what do I do?

"Maria?"

"Yeah."

"Conner *is* going tonight," Elizabeth said.

"Oh. Well, then maybe I . . . no. You know what? I'll go anyway," Maria said.

"You will?" Elizabeth asked, trying not to sound desperate. How was she going to deal with both of them?

"Yeah. I'm not going to ruin my social life because I can't get over Conner. I'm going to have some fun."

At least one of us is, Elizabeth thought.

The phone rang, jarring Conner as he tried to concentrate on his physics homework. He'd thought Elizabeth was still on the line.

"Hello?" Conner said.

"Hey. It's Andy."

"Hey, man."

"I've been commissioned by Tia the cruise director to force you into coming to the Riot tonight," Andy said.

"No need," Conner said, leaning back in his chair. "I'll be there."

His door flew open, and Elizabeth stood there, hand on hip.

"Hold on, Andy," Conner said. He held the

mouthpiece to his chest. "Do you knock?" he asked Elizabeth.

"You don't."

"So . . ."

"Maria's coming tonight," Elizabeth said.

"So?" Conner repeated.

"Well, if you're still gonna go, then I'm not gonna go," Elizabeth said.

"Why?" Conner asked.

"Because I'm going to feel guilty and then I won't have any fun, so what's the point?" Elizabeth said.

"Has anyone ever told you you're insane?" Conner asked.

"All the time," Elizabeth said with a smirk.

Conner brought the phone to his ear. "Andy? Change of plans. I'm not going."

"Wait a minute. I didn't mean—," Elizabeth said. Conner held his hand up to her.

"Tia's going to kill you, dude," Andy said.

"I'll deal with Tia," Conner said. "There are other women involved who are a lot harder to deal with than her."

Elizabeth's face reddened, and she slammed the door. Conner smiled.

"What was that?" Andy asked.

"Nothing," Conner replied. "Just the wind."

Elizabeth and Maria were barely through the door at the Riot when Tia grabbed their wrists and pulled them toward the crowded dance floor.

"This place is in serious need of your help," she yelled over the music. "The dancing has been totally lame."

"Can I at least get my jacket off?" Elizabeth shouted, squinting through the smoke-filled darkness at Tia's green lamé tank top. She laughed as Tia swung her hips to the pulsing music, then coughed when the secondhand smoke hit her throat.

"Oh, fine!" Tia said, pretending to mope. "Our table's over here." She started weaving through the maze of stools and silver-topped tables in the seating area, deftly dodging other hyper Riot goers. Elizabeth followed, her eyes still adjusting to the throbbing lights as Maria trailed behind. Tia turned around and stood behind the black, rail-backed chair where Andy was sitting, and Elizabeth noticed that Tia was practically covered in glitter from her eyelids to her shoulders.

"Nice makeup job," Elizabeth said, shrugging out of her newish leather jacket. Even though the air-conditioning was always going full blast, the Riot was a perpetual psychedelic sauna. Elizabeth was already starting to sweat.

"She's feeling really sparkly," Andy said, his blue eyes shining.

Tia just grinned, moving her shoulders slightly to the continuous beat. "Where's Jessica?"

"She didn't feel like dancing," Elizabeth said, hanging her jacket on the back of a chair.

"We have got to do something about that girl," Tia said. "Soon. But in the meantime Angel just went up to the bar to get me a diet something. Do you guys want anything? He's catchable."

"I'd love a diet something," Elizabeth said, taking the seat across from Andy. She had to pull herself up against the table to keep from mashing shoulders with the grungy guy behind her.

"Regular for me," Maria said, sliding into the seat next to Elizabeth.

Tia grimaced playfully. "Regular Coke, Maria? You sure? I hear you can cut rust with that stuff."

Maria laughed. "You don't even want to know what's in the diet stuff, Tia."

Elizabeth was surprised and relieved at the sound of Maria's laughter. She hadn't heard it all day.

"All right, I'm on it. No dancing till I get back," Tia said, pointing at them to punctuate her demand.

"We wouldn't think it," Elizabeth called after her. She leaned in toward Maria. "So, listen, Conner decided not to come," Elizabeth stage-whispered to be heard above the music.

"Thank God!" Maria responded. "I'm just going to relax and have a good time."

Me too, Elizabeth thought, attempting to lean back before she realized she had no place to go.

"So, did you see Tia's shoes? They're, like, four-inch

95

heels," Maria said, her brown eyes wide. "How does she dance in those things?"

"I think she practices alone in her room at night," Andy said, taking a sip of his ginger ale. "It's a height-envy thing."

"Oh, yeah?" Maria said, lowering one eyebrow. "So where are *your* heels?"

Andy sat up straighter, adjusting the collar on his white oxford shirt. "Hey, anyone would have an inadequacy complex around you, Amazon woman."

Maria laughed. "I just love looking down at the world."

Elizabeth and Andy groaned, and Elizabeth crumpled up a clean cocktail napkin and threw it at her friend.

"You don't have to rub it in, supermodel," Elizabeth said, admiring Maria's black boat-neck sweater and matching miniskirt. She looked amazing, but anything looked amazing on Maria's five-foot, eleven-inch frame.

Elizabeth leaned her elbows on the table and stared out over the crowd, perfectly content to let Maria become the center of attention. For the first time all day, Elizabeth felt comfortable. She'd gotten away from Conner, and Maria seemed to be perking up. Maybe she'd actually be able to focus on having a good time.

Elizabeth spotted Tia and Angel approaching their table, each carrying two drinks. She waved at

Angel, and he grinned, lifting his chin to acknowledge her. As usual, Angel looked totally hip and incredibly handsome. His red, retro T-shirt looked striking against his deep ebony skin, and his smile was gorgeous enough to send Elizabeth's heart skipping.

"Hey, guys," Angel said as he placed the drinks in the middle of the table. "Drink up before Tia explodes from unexpended energy."

Tia stood, hovering over the table, bouncing slightly as she sipped her soda. Elizabeth laughed and glanced over at Maria, but her friend was staring at the main entrance to the Riot, and she didn't look happy. In fact, *shock* was the first word that came to Elizabeth's mind.

She followed Maria's line of sight, hoping she wasn't going to see who she thought she was going to see. But there he was. Conner McDermott was closing in on their table in one of those should've-been-in-slow-motion moments—his intense green eyes focused on Elizabeth as he strolled effortlessly through the throng.

"Well, well, well!" Tia declared sarcastically, "Look who decided to come out of hiding."

Conner half smiled at Tia and then looked directly at Elizabeth. "It suddenly occurred to me that you can't hide forever."

Elizabeth wanted to melt into the floor. That little phrase didn't bode well.

"Hey, man." Conner knocked fists with Angel, pecked Tia on the cheek, and then pulled up a chair, positioning himself between Andy and Elizabeth. Miraculously, everyone at the table behind them had vacated.

"Antisocial Man," Andy greeted him with a nod. His eyes were darting between Elizabeth and Maria. Elizabeth realized with a sickening dread that Andy knew about the little love triangle. She wondered if Conner had confided in him or if he'd figured it out himself.

Elizabeth reached for her drink, knocking Conner's elbow, and then yanked back her hand as if she'd been stung. Her face was on fire as she tried to figure out what to do with her arms. She suddenly felt like her every move was being scrutinized by everyone around her. Finally she gave up on her drink and clasped her hands under the table. Looking unaffected was very hard work.

"Hey, Maria," Conner said.

Maria smiled shyly. "Hey."

Okay, so they were sort of talking. *Please just don't let Conner do anything stupid.* He shifted in his seat and removed his worn suede jacket. As he hung it over the back of his chair, his bare arm brushed Elizabeth's, and goose bumps popped up on her skin.

"So, Conner," Andy said, acting suave as he ran a hand over his red curls, "what changed your mind? My magnetic personality?"

"Megan decided to have a small army of sopho-more girls over. Here seemed as good a place as any to escape," Conner answered. He looked at Elizabeth and held her gaze until she blushed.

Elizabeth's heart pounded furiously. If he kept doing that, Maria was going to catch on in no time. Her best friend wasn't stupid. Elizabeth attempted to scoot her chair farther away from Conner but bumped into Maria's chair. She was trapped.

"Sorry," Elizabeth muttered. She thought she saw a flicker of suspicion in Maria's eyes.

That's it, Elizabeth thought. *I can't take this any-more. I'm telling her tonight. Here if I have to.*

"Are you okay, Liz?" Tia asked. "You look sick all of a sudden."

"I'm fine," Elizabeth said, wrapping her arms around herself as if she could pull her body in tighter and avoid touching Conner again. Suddenly the music seemed ridiculously loud and intense. Beads of sweat broke out along Elizabeth's hairline as she tried to lean closer to Maria without making it obvious.

"Well, maybe some dancing will help," Tia said, placing her empty glass on the table. "Let's go."

Elizabeth was perfectly ready to disappear inside the gyrating throng of dancers. But the moment she pushed back her chair to get up, the music stopped.

"All right, everybody, we're gonna slow it down just

a little bit," the deejay said. "Let you catch your breath."

Elizabeth whimpered internally. Maybe she could make a break for the bathroom.

"What?" Tia said as the opening strains of a slow song poured through the speakers. "But I *have* my breath. I have tons of breath!"

"Come on, baby," Angel said, taking her by the hand. "It'll be like a warm-up."

Elizabeth made a point of watching Angel and Tia until they got to the dance floor. Conner was staring at her profile, and she felt like he was boring holes in her face. Then he shifted in his seat. His knee pressed against her leg, and it was all she could do to keep from screaming. He leaned toward her, and she knew what was coming. But she had zero time to think of a response.

"Want to dance?" Conner asked her. He had just had a breath mint.

Elizabeth closed her eyes. How could he do this to her? How could he put her in this position? Oh, but she really, *really* wanted to dance with him. Maria was staring at her, mouth open in surprise.

"Liz?" His voice was all deep and throaty. It sent a chill down her spine.

"Well, I'm dying of suspense," Andy said, breaking the stillness. It gave Elizabeth exactly the kick she needed.

Her chair scraped back as she stood up. "I need a new drink," she announced.

Conner pointed to Elizabeth's glass. "Your glass is half full."

Yeah, and your head is half empty, Elizabeth thought.

"It's flat," she said, leveling him with a glare. Of course, it had no effect on Conner. He just stared right back, clearly amused.

"I'll go with you," Maria said, standing. She grabbed Elizabeth's hand and started moving into the flow of people heading for the bar and bathrooms.

Maria and Elizabeth were both silent as they jostled their way through the crowd and up the winding staircase to the second-floor bar. At the top of the stairs Maria finally turned around, a heated, angry look on her face.

"What was that?" she demanded.

Elizabeth was sure the whole club could hear her heart pounding. "What was what?" she asked lamely.

"Conner," Maria said. "I can't even believe he just asked you to dance in front of me. My best friend! Is that just his way of trying to upset me?"

"Um . . ." Elizabeth grasped for a response.

"Well, it worked." Maria crossed her arms over her chest. "Why does he have this need to hurt me?" she asked, tears in her voice.

All right. Enough was enough. "Maria, about Conner . . . ," Elizabeth said, screwing up her courage.

"Oh God, Liz," Maria said, reaching out and

grasping Elizabeth's wrist. "I'm so sorry I keep talking about this. It must be getting so old."

"No, that's okay," Elizabeth said. "It's just—"

"Thanks for being there for me through this whole thing. I mean, really, I can't believe I accused you of liking him this morning." She laughed. "I must be really losing it."

Elizabeth's stomach churned.

"You're such a good friend, Liz," Maria said. She wrapped her arms around Elizabeth's shoulders and held her in a hug. Elizabeth hugged her back, holding in tears of frustration.

Maria pulled away and smiled at Elizabeth. "No more Conner talk tonight. I'm going to go get some drinks."

Elizabeth briefly considered trying again, but she felt like she'd been drained of energy. "Okay."

"Listen," Maria said, "the bar is packed. Why don't you wait for me over by the balcony? You look like you need some air."

Elizabeth smiled wanly. *Maybe I'll just throw myself off the balcony.*

Conner stared at the shadowy crowd as Andy carried on a conversation with some random guy who'd stopped at their table. He couldn't believe Elizabeth had blown him off like that. And why was it that she was more sexy when she was being frustrating?

He pushed back from the table and started to maneuver around behind Andy's chair. Just sitting here waiting was driving him crazy.

"Where're you going, man?" Andy asked.

"Bathroom," Conner answered. "Want anything?"

"From the bathroom?" Andy asked, cracking a smile.

Conner just rolled his eyes and kept moving. His eyes flicked toward the first-level bar, but he didn't see Maria anywhere. She was too tall to miss, even in a mob. He headed for the stairs. On the way up, the flow of traffic came to a complete stop three times as people did the socializing thing, hooking up with others who were on their way down. Conner breathed deeply to control his frustration. *It's a good thing I really didn't have to go to the bathroom,* he thought. *I never would have made it.*

"Hi, Conner."

He glanced up and saw a pretty brunette descending the stairs.

He nodded, racking his brain for her name. Betsy, maybe. No, Beth? Something starting with a *B.* She was in his calculus class. No, maybe it was English. Whichever, he wasn't interested.

"See ya," she said in a hopeful voice as she passed. Conner smiled noncommittally and moved on.

He noticed several other girls checking him out as he made his way through the second-floor minglers. He'd worn his favorite black T-shirt, and he knew he looked good. But he hadn't worn it for any of them. There was only one person he was interested in tempting.

And there she was.

Elizabeth was standing with her back to him, leaning on the balcony railing and staring out over the dance floor below. Conner took a moment to admire her lean silhouette. She was wearing a pair of slim-fitting, cranberry-colored pants and a satiny tank top. Conner could practically feel the cool fabric on his fingertips. He had to touch her.

Conner came up behind Elizabeth and slipped his arms around her waist. "You're gonna have to stop running away from me," he said, touching his cheek to her enticingly bare neck.

Elizabeth whirled around and pushed him away. "What's your problem?" she demanded.

Conner's eyes narrowed. "*My* problem?"

"Yes, your problem," Elizabeth hissed, her face flushed. "Maria's right over there."

Conner was getting tired of having Maria's location mapped out for him every five minutes, but he also didn't feel like arguing about her. He ran his fingers down Elizabeth's arm and smiled as she closed her eyes at his touch. He held her hand lightly. "That's why we're going upstairs," Conner said, tugging on her hand.

"We are?" she whispered, blinking up at him.

He nodded and took her other hand, pulling her away from the railing.

"Wait a minute," she said, snapping to. "No, we're not." She tried to pull her hands away, but Conner held her tightly. "I have to wait for her," Elizabeth said.

Conner released one hand and put his finger to her lips. Elizabeth's eyelids fluttered, and he knew he had her. "Come on, Elizabeth," he said. "If we don't go right now, she might turn around and see us standing here holding hands."

Her beautiful blue-green eyes were a swirl of confusion and longing. "I—"

He leaned forward and pressed his cheek against hers. Her skin was so soft, and the scent of her hair made him tense with anticipation. He felt her body weaken. "Come upstairs with me, Liz. I promise you won't regret it."

Elizabeth blindly followed Conner up the stairs to the third floor. The dark floor. The make-out floor.

How had she let this happen? She was abandoning Maria. But it was hard to think of anything with Conner's fingers entangled with hers and the feel of his breath on her ear still lingering. At that moment she probably would have followed him anywhere, even though a very, very loud voice in the back of her head was screaming at her to walk away.

When they reached the top of the stairs, Elizabeth looked around slowly as though caught in a fog. They called it the Riot Lounge, but everybody knew it as the make-out floor. It was Elizabeth's first time here, but she could instantly see what attracted privacy-seeking pairs. Cozy, wine-colored circular booths lined the walls, and the room was lit solely by flickering candles. An old jazz tune wafted from the speakers, somehow drowning out the throbbing music from the dance floor two stories below. There were lip-locked couples everywhere.

Elizabeth's heart slammed against her chest as Conner led her to a very dark corner. He held his hand out in an "after you" gesture.

A million thoughts ricocheted through Elizabeth's mind. Had he brought Maria here? In fact, how many girls had he brought here? Was she actually losing her mind? Even so, Elizabeth only hesitated a moment.

Conner's hand slid to the small of her back and eased her into the booth. He crawled in after her, pulled her close, and brushed a few stray strands of hair out of her face. The touch of his fingertips was enough to make her melt, and she didn't put up a fight when he pulled her face toward him.

"You are so beautiful," she heard him murmur. Then their lips met, and Elizabeth ceased to think at all.

Andy Marsden

I give up.

I've told Maria to get over Conner. I've suggested to Conner to just admit he has a thing for Liz. I haven't said anything to Liz about telling Maria how she feels about Conner, but that's only because Elizabeth hasn't told _me_ she has a thing for Conner. I just figured it out on my own.

So, right now, there's just nothing I can do.

I've said it before and I'll say it again. Those three are a living, breathing soap opera. But it's getting more painful to watch by the day.

It is pretty funny watching Conner trip all over himself for a girl, though . . . _finally._

CHAPTER 7

Throwing It all away

In his dream Jeremy stood on the beach with Jessica Wakefield. The sunset danced bright oranges and reds on her blond hair, and a great ska band played somewhere in the distance. She reached out and held his hand. Jeremy could feel the cool, dry sand between his toes and smell the soft scent of Jessica's perfume. She was so beautiful in her yellow sundress and stethoscope—wait a minute—a stethoscope?

"Jeremy? Are you home, honey?" His mother's voice. Suddenly his mother was on the beach also, her keys in hand—

That was when Jeremy heard the buzzing. It was humming in his ears like demon-possessed bumblebees.

"What is that sound?" His mother again. "Is that the oven timer?"

Jeremy rubbed his eyes. What had happened to the beach? And why was the oven timer going off?

"Dinner!" Jeremy jumped out of his chair, nearly collapsing on his right leg, which had completely fallen asleep.

"You made dinner? Jeremy, that's so sweet," his mother said, walking over to the stove. Jeremy was still getting his bearings. He couldn't believe he'd passed out in a kitchen chair. They were the most uncomfortable things on earth. The moment he had the thought, a sharp pain jabbed him in the back.

"Actually, you made dinner," Jeremy said. "I just reheated the leftover lasagna." He leaned against the cool Formica counter as his mother pulled the baking pan out of the oven.

"Did I burn it?" he asked. Life was returning to his leg, and he was experiencing a major pins-and-needles attack. He banged his foot against the floor to clear them.

"It looks perfect, actually," Mrs. Aames said. She placed the steaming pan on top of the stove and smiled at Jeremy. "Unlike you and me." She pushed a shock of limp, dark hair behind her ear.

"Did you get any sleep?" Jeremy asked, stifling a yawn.

"A little," she answered. "Where are the girls?"

"I made them some macaroni and cheese a few hours ago. They're zoned out in front of some Disney video upstairs. They might even be asleep. I haven't heard any screaming fights recently."

"That's the best news I've heard all day," Mrs. Aames said, pulling a couple of forks and knives out of a drawer.

"Was Dad feeling any better when you left?" Jeremy asked, stifling a yawn.

"Much," Margaret Aames said, slicing into the lasagna. "Dr. Fetters said your father is going to be fine. He might even be able to come home as early as tomorrow. He just needs to take it easy. Tests show the attack wasn't as bad as it seemed."

"That's good news," Jeremy said. He handed his mother the plates he'd taken out earlier. "But if it wasn't that bad, why was he out cold all night?"

"He was exhausted," Mrs. Aames said. "His body's been through a lot. The doctor said he's going to need to take some blood-pressure medication and something for stress."

Jeremy's brow creased in concern. "Well, I'm sure the doctor knows what Dad needs."

Mrs. Aames dug out a piece of lasagna and slapped it on a plate. "What your father needs is to get a job."

"What?" Jeremy exclaimed, feeling the fog in his head quickly lift. He narrowed his eyes at his mother, wondering if the lack of sleep had affected her brain.

But she simply raised her eyebrows at him and shrugged one slim shoulder. "What, what?" she said, handing him his dinner.

Jeremy put the plate down on the counter. "Mom, how can you even *think* of Dad trying to get work now? You just said he had to take it easy. I mean, trying to get a job was what gave him the heart attack in the first place." This was obvious logic, right? Had she not lived here for the past few months?

Margaret Aames smiled wearily at her son. "No, honey, it's the *not* working, the *not* providing, that stressed out your father," she said calmly. "It made him feel as if he had failed. I just hope this heart attack will wake him up and make him realize how bad things have gotten. Maybe now he'll get off the couch."

"How can you say that? Who *are* you?" Jeremy shook his head in disbelief. The subdued, determined tone in his mother's voice actually sent chills down his spine. He stared into her eyes, half expecting to find them hard and cruel. But instead they were as warm and kind as always.

"Jeremy, you're not listening to me," Mrs. Aames said evenly.

"I'm listening—I just can't believe what I'm hearing," Jeremy barked. "Dad needs us to take care of him right now. He needs rest."

"Of course he does, in the short term. I'm just saying—"

"I can't listen to this," Jeremy said, suddenly feeling as if the room were shrinking in around him. He grabbed his varsity jacket off the back of the chair. "I'm leaving. Tell Trisha and Emma I said good night. I'm going to the hospital."

"Jeremy, at least eat something first," his mother said, sounding resigned.

But Jeremy was already out the door. He drove five miles above the speed limit all the way to the hospital—fast enough to keep him sane, but not fast enough to get a ticket.

Jeremy found intensive care easily. He had gotten the floor plan down pat after spending the entire night hitting all the coffee and snack vending machines within a quarter mile of the ICU. He didn't even check in with the nurses. He just went straight to his father's side and listened to his labored breathing.

"It's gonna be okay, Dad," he said. "I'm gonna make sure you get better."

As Jeremy stared at the screen on his father's heart monitor, his vision started to blur. He leaned back in his chair to sleep, but the moment he closed his eyes, he saw Coach Anderson. He remembered how angry the coach had been when Jeremy had called and said he had a family emergency and couldn't make the game. Then he saw Ally, his manager at House of Java, and immediately started wondering how she was going to react when he called to say he couldn't come to work tomorrow. He'd just begged her for more hours a few days ago, and now he was going to leave her shorthanded.

And then he saw Jessica. She probably hated him by now. In her eyes he'd just let her run off in tears and hadn't even come after her. He hadn't stopped by. He hadn't called.

She must think I'm so shallow, Jeremy thought. He wrenched open his eyes and picked up the phone to call her, but then he realized it was the middle of the night. And his brain was so fogged, he couldn't remember her number anyway.

Tomorrow, he thought. *Tomorrow I'll fix everything.* Right now it was time to pass out.

"It's totally lame out here," Cherie said, looking out over the glittering pool in Josh's backyard. "Everyone's just sitting around talking."

Melissa took a sip of her soda and leaned back in the soft, blue-and-white-striped lounge chair. "I kind of like it," she said, looking up at the pitch-black night sky. "It's peaceful."

The patio area was also Will-free, which made it much easier for Melissa to breathe. Just knowing he was here somewhere kept her heart pounding uncomfortably and the thin sheen of sweat ever present on her palms.

"Right. But this is a party, Melissa," Gina said. She leaned forward in her seat and ducked her head to check her shimmery toenail polish. "Parties aren't supposed to be peaceful."

"I think we should go inside and dance," Cherie said, pushing her thick, auburn curls behind her shoulders. She stood up and pulled down on the hem of her white eyelet dress. It was still dangerously short, but that was the way Cherie liked her skirts. "I didn't spend over an hour defrizzing to waste this hair on you guys."

"I'm with her," Gina said. She pulled a compact out of her minibag and checked her precision-perfect eye makeup before she stood. "Come on, Melissa. Where's your inner party girl?"

She no longer exists, Melissa thought. "You know what? You guys go. I'm just gonna stay here."

Gina and Cherie shot each other a concerned glance. "Melissa, is everything okay?" Cherie asked.

"Everything's fine," Melissa answered with a tight smile, wishing they would just leave her alone. She didn't even know why she had agreed to come tonight. Wait. Yes, she did. She'd come to keep up appearances. If she didn't go to a huge victory party for a game of which Will had been the star, everyone would suspect something was wrong. And Melissa couldn't have that. She couldn't deal with explaining. Not yet.

The back door of the house opened, and the music blared out into the yard. Melissa grimaced. It was the song the El Carro cheerleading squad had danced to for their halftime routine last year—a dance Melissa had choreographed herself. She knew what was coming.

"Come on, Melissa," Gina said, grabbing her wrist. "You *have* to dance with us."

"You guys—"

"No. You can't turn us down," Cherie said, taking Melissa's other arm. "It's tradition."

Melissa briefly thought about pulling back, but she didn't want to make a scene. She followed Cherie and Gina through the den and into the living room, trying hard to keep her chin up and her shoulders back. If Will saw her, she wanted him to think that she was fine. That she was over it.

Cherie strutted right into the middle of the room, and Melissa and Gina followed. Renee Talbot, another El Carro cheerleader, joined them, and Melissa managed a small smile. Normally she thrived on a moment like this. Living it up with her friends, carrying on an old, silly El Carro tradition, but all she could bring herself to do was move her hips slightly to the beat. She knew Will was in the room somewhere, watching her. Pitying her.

When the song ended, Cherie, Gina, and Renee clapped and screamed, and Melissa smiled at them. She was about to turn around and escape back to the pool area when a slow song came on. At the moment she heard the opening guitar strains, she spotted Will and froze. He was talking with Matt on the outskirts of the crowd, but he saw her out of the corner of his eye. Will paused in the middle of his conversation and looked directly at her, his expression unreadable. For a split second she thought he might actually ask her to dance. But then he returned his attention to his friend.

Melissa turned away and started to push through the crowd. Couples were pairing off and moving slowly to the music, making it difficult to get through without knocking anyone over. Then, a moment before she was free, Melissa heard Cherie calling her name.

"Melissa! Wait a second!"

She spun around, ready to tell Cherie that she was going home, but the words died in her throat. Cherie was dragging a protesting Will across the room toward her. Melissa's vision clouded over black, and she knew she was about to faint. She reached out and grabbed an arm, oblivious to who she was holding on to.

"Cherie, what are you doing?" Melissa whispered.

Melissa watched as her best friend jostled Will into place right in front of her. His face was bright red. "I don't know what's going on with you two, but I know you haven't spoken all night," Cherie said. "So I want you to kiss and make up right now. This is a party! And you know you're just going to make up tomorrow anyway."

Melissa felt tears sting the corners of her eyes. She knew Cherie was just trying to help, but the girl had no idea what she was talking about. *She doesn't know because you didn't tell her,* a nagging voice reminded her. She looked around and noticed that all of their friends were in the near vicinity, either watching or at least listening in. Josh, Matt, Lila,

Gina, Amy, Seth Hiller. *What do I do?* Melissa wondered, wishing she could just disappear.

Will leaned toward her, and her breath caught in her throat. "You didn't tell them?" he whispered. "Not even Cherie?"

Melissa shook her head almost imperceptibly. "Will, just dance with me. Just once. Then she'll leave us alone," she whispered desperately.

Will pulled back and sighed, his eyes full of sorrow. "I can't, Liss," he said quietly. "I would, but . . . I can't keep doing this. I can't keep coming back."

Melissa's heart plummeted.

"What are you guys whispering about?" Cherie demanded loudly. Will shot her a menacing glance, and Cherie rolled her eyes but looked away.

"What do you mean, you can't keep coming back?" Melissa asked. "We just broke up this morning."

Will's posture stiffened, and he looked at her warily. A cold, sick feeling of dread slipped down Melissa's spine as realization finally seeped through.

"You've been planning this," she said, in a louder voice than she intended. She took a step back as her friends all dropped their own peripheral conversations.

Will looked her directly in the eye. "Melissa, calm down," he said. "Maybe we should go outside. We can find somewhere to talk." He reached out a hand to her, but she knocked it away.

"I don't want to go outside," she said through clenched teeth, no longer aware of the crowd or the music or the heat. All she could see was Will's steadily paling face. "How long?" she asked. "How long have you been planning to dump me?"

There was an audible gasp from the spectator circle. Melissa barely noticed. "Melissa, please," Will said. "You don't want to do this."

"How long?" Melissa shouted, the tears brimming over.

Will didn't answer. He just stood there staring at her, all concerned and pitying. He felt bad for her. How sweet. He felt bad that she was standing in the middle of a crowded room, crumbling like a bag of potato chips, all because he'd broken her heart.

Suddenly Melissa felt Cherie's arm slip around her shoulders, and the room came into focus. Lila and Amy were whispering in the corner, and dozens of people were staring at her, then blinking and looking away the moment her eyes lit upon them. They were all talking about her. And now they all knew what a pathetic loser she was.

And it was her own fault. She'd let them all into her nightmare—opened herself up for public ridicule.

"Melissa," Cherie said. "Maybe we should—"

"I have to go," Melissa said quietly, shrugging from Cherie's grasp.

"Let me drive you," Gina said, stepping forward.

"No, I got it," Melissa said, holding up a hand. Gina froze as if Melissa were wielding a gun.

Hold it together, Melissa told herself. *Just get out of here and everything will be . . . will be . . .* But she couldn't finish the sentence. Everything was not going to be fine. Ever.

Melissa cast one last humiliated look at Will and then turned and stumbled out into the darkness.

It could have been hours, it could have been minutes, but Elizabeth wasn't really paying attention to the time. Kissing Conner was too distracting, too wonderful, too overwhelming, too perfect.

Perfect. Until ten seconds of bone-jarring feedback shot through the stereo system. It was all the time needed for a few hits of reality to pass through Elizabeth's heavily kissed haze.

She broke away from Conner, blinking in an attempt to clear her brain.

"What's the matter?" Conner asked, tracing her ear with light kisses.

Elizabeth closed her eyes. "I have to get back downstairs," she said.

"No, you don't," Conner whispered.

"Yes, I do," Elizabeth said. She didn't move a muscle. "Maria's probably looking for me."

"So? She has other friends," Conner said. Elizabeth moaned in frustration as his lips danced down her neck.

"Conner, come on," Elizabeth said, pressing her hand against his chest. It had no effect except to make his kisses more insistent. "Please. Maria—"

Conner pulled back. "No, not Maria." He pointed to himself. "Conner."

"Very funny." She used his sudden slight distance to try to slide toward the end of the booth. Unfortunately she had forgotten that Conner had his arm firmly around her waist.

Elizabeth sighed and looked him in the eye. "Am I gonna have to scream?"

He raised one eyebrow. "You wouldn't."

"You don't know me that well," Elizabeth said, staring him down.

"All right, let's both go," Conner said, releasing his grip and emerging from the other side of the booth in one fluid motion.

"Wait a minute!" Elizabeth said, jumping up. She straightened her blouse quickly and grabbed Conner's wrist.

"Changed your mind?" Conner asked, smiling suggestively.

Okay, Elizabeth thought, but she shook her head. "No. It's just . . . we can't go down there together." Conner stared at her blankly. "She'll know," Elizabeth said.

Conner tugged his hand out of Elizabeth's grip and crossed his arms over his chest. "This is getting old," he said.

"I know, but she's my best friend—"

"If you're so worried about Maria, why don't you just tell her what's going on?" Conner interrupted, his voice rising slightly, attracting a few glances from nearby couples.

"Because it would kill her," Elizabeth said through clenched teeth.

Conner shrugged. "Maybe, but she's going to find out eventually anyway," he whispered back.

Elizabeth blinked. She got really dizzy, really fast. Eventually? Did that mean that Conner actually wanted this . . . whatever it was . . . to last?

"Liz?" Conner's voice only partly registered past the reeling inside her head.

Eventually?

"Liz!"

"What?"

"Are you gonna tell her?" Conner asked, raising his eyebrows.

Elizabeth looked around the room, feeling conspicuous. They were standing and talking in an otherwise quiet room of intimate couples. People were starting to stir. "Conner," Elizabeth said, as quietly as possible. "It's really . . . sweet of you to be concerned about Maria, and I know the fact that I keep bringing her up is probably really annoying. . . ."

She waited for him to deny it, but he didn't. Elizabeth stood up a little straighter, feeling defiant.

"But you don't know Maria like I do," she said. "I have to handle this my way."

Conner's eyes clouded over. "You're not handling it at all."

"But I will," Elizabeth said firmly. She stepped past him and paused, glancing over her shoulder at his rigid back. He was angry, but there was nothing she could do about that right now. "Just wait five minutes before you come down, okay?" she asked.

"No. I think I'll go down first," Conner said, turning around and fixing Elizabeth with a hardened glare. "I have this sudden urge to get the hell out of here."

Conner brushed past her and pounded down the steps, leaving Elizabeth standing conspicuously alone in the center of the lounge. She ducked her head and slid back into their booth to wait. The seat was still warm from their presence, but Elizabeth suddenly felt very cold.

Senior Poll Category #1: Class Couple

Please make only one nomination.

Conner McDermott
Who cares?

Maria Slater
~~Maria Slater and Conner McDermott~~
Will Simmons and Melissa Fox

Elizabeth Wakefield
~~Elizabeth Wakefield and Conner McDermott~~

Ken Matthews
I have no idea.

TIA RAMIREZ
WILL SIMMONS AND MELISSA FOX

<u>Andy Marsden</u>
Will Simmons and Melissa Fox

<u>melissa Fox</u>
melissa Fox and Will Simmons

<u>Will Simmons</u>
Oh, no.

<u>Jessica Wakefield</u>
Anyone but Will Simmons and Melissa Fox

CHAPTER 8
Love and the Closet Rebel

Melissa whipped her mother's Lexus into the driveway and slammed on the brakes, screeching the car to a stop inches from the garage door. She looked over at her father's BMW and grimaced. Her parents hadn't left yet. That meant that on top of public humiliation, she was going to have to deal with—

"Melissa Candice Fox!"

Good old Mom, Melissa thought as she glared through the windshield. Her mother stalked along the front walk, beaded evening gown and all. Melissa threw open the car door, slammed it behind her, and started walking, determined to get past her mother.

"What do you think you're doing?" her mother demanded, grabbing Melissa's arm. Melissa yanked herself free and kept walking. She wasn't surprised when her mother refused to take the hint. She scurried along behind Melissa, her beads clicking as she went.

"That's right, just walk away," Mrs. Fox said, following Melissa into the house. "Well, don't think you're ever driving my car again, young lady."

"Like I care," Melissa shot back, whirling around in the middle of the entryway.

"What are you doing home?" Mrs. Fox asked, slamming the front door behind her. Melissa tried not to wince as the painting on the wall behind her mother shook from the impact. "What's got you driving like a maniac?"

"Will dumped me, Mom. Happy now?" Melissa asked. She lifted her chin and stared her mother down, defying her to say what she was so obviously going to say.

"He dumped you?" Mrs. Fox asked, paling slightly. "Melissa, what did you do?"

Melissa's heart shattered into a thousand pieces even though she'd known it was coming. Why did she always have to feel it so much even though her mother never surprised her? She felt her hands clench into tight fists, her fingernails cutting into her soft palms.

"Why do you do that, Mom?" Melissa asked, tears spilling onto her warm cheeks. "Why do you always do that?"

"Do what?" her mother demanded. "What did I do to you now?"

"You always blame me," Melissa choked out, barely able to catch her breath. A little voice in the back of her head told her not to bother. It wasn't like her mom was going to hear her anyway.

Melissa felt her father walk into the foyer behind her. "What's going on?" he asked.

"Will broke up with Melissa," Mrs. Fox said tersely.

"Oh, honey, I'm sorry," Mr. Fox said. Melissa felt his hand on her shoulder and turned to look up at him. Her father was so handsome in his tuxedo, with his brown hair all combed back. Melissa wished he would just stay home with her for once. Sit on the couch and watch TV with her like when she was little. But he was never around. Not even on weekends. It occurred to her as he smiled sympathetically that she hadn't even seen him in two weeks.

Mr. Fox pulled a handkerchief out of his pocket and handed it to Melissa. "Remember, honey," he said in a deep, consoling voice. "Everything happens for a reason."

Melissa's heart dropped into her shoes, and she took a step back. "You don't even have a clue, Dad," she said. "Neither one of you does." She looked back and forth between her parents. They were staring at her blankly as if they were looking at some caged animal in a zoo. "Why don't you both just leave?" Melissa said, narrowing her swollen eyes at her mother. "I know you're just wondering when the ungrateful daughter's going to quit blubbering so you can go."

"Now, Melissa—"

"Shut up, Mom."

Her mother's face was a mask of anger. "You're grounded."

"There's a shocker," Melissa said, starting up the thickly carpeted stairs. She grasped the wooden banister for support.

"For a month."

It doesn't matter, Melissa thought. *Just keep walking.*

"Come on, Roger," Mrs. Fox said. Melissa heard the front door open. "There's no point to this."

No point, Melissa repeated to herself. *Just go. Leave me here alone.*

She heard the door click shut, and without warning, a sob escaped from her throat. Then Melissa collapsed on the top step and cried like she would never stop.

Conner felt his way blindly along the uneven hedge that lined the backyard at Tia's house. He'd taken this shortcut a million times but hardly ever at two in the morning when there wasn't even a shred of moonlight to guide the way.

Something caught at his jeans, and Conner tripped. He put out his hand to break the fall, and a sharp rock pressed into his palm. Shaking out his hand, Conner took a deep breath, hoping to calm his racing heart.

"Dammit, McDermott," he whispered. "What are you doing here?"

He briefly considered turning around and heading

back to his own house, but he'd already come through five yards and past one possibly rabid dog to get here. Besides, going home meant going back to bed five feet away from Elizabeth, and he couldn't handle being around her right now. Okay, so there was a bathroom between them, but even that couldn't keep him from imagining her in there, cuddled up under the white comforter in that little nightshirt she liked so much.

Inching forward, Conner finally found the break in the hedge and slipped through, then rushed across the yard to Tia's window as quietly as possible. The last thing Conner wanted to do was disturb Mr. Ramirez from his sleep. The man had a shotgun and wasn't afraid to use it. At least that was what he'd said the last time he caught Conner sneaking through his yard after hours.

Conner reached out and tapped Tia's bedroom window. It slid open almost instantly, causing Conner to jump back.

"What are you doing here?" Tia whispered.

"You scared the hell out of me," Conner said. "What're you doing up?"

"I'm not up—I'm a light sleeper," Tia answered, pulling her flannel pajama top tightly around her body. "What's up? Is something wrong?"

"Kind of. Can I come in?" Conner asked, placing his hand on the windowsill.

Tia slapped it away and looked over her shoulder at her bedroom door. "No. I'll come out. Just give me a sec."

Conner stepped back as Tia silently closed the window. He shoved his hands into the front pockets of his jeans and walked toward the back door. A cool breeze ruffled his hair and caused goose bumps to break out on his arms, even with his suede jacket over his T-shirt.

The glass door to the kitchen slid open, and Tia shuffled out. She was wearing a pair of fuzzy pink slippers and had pulled an afghan over her shoulders.

"Let's sit on the swings," Tia said. "Less chance they'll hear us."

Conner followed her over to the rickety swing set, where they used to play when they were kids. Tia plopped down on a swing, and Conner tried to follow suit, but it took some effort to wedge himself into the small seat.

"Comfy?" Tia asked, grinning.

"Very." Conner grimaced. He crossed his arms over his chest, shoving his hands under his elbows for warmth.

"So spill," Tia said. "To what do I owe the honor of this midnight rendezvous?"

Conner glanced at her out of the corner of his eye. "Don't freak," he said.

"Okay," she answered tentatively.

Conner took a deep breath and blew it out in a short burst. "I've been sort of . . . fooling around with Elizabeth."

"I knew it!" Tia squealed happily. Then she slapped her hand over her mouth as Conner warily checked her parents' window for signs of life. Nothing.

"I knew it," she repeated in a whisper, spinning her swing and leaning toward him. "I knew you guys would hook up."

"Yeah? Well, I wish you had warned me," Conner said, twisting the chains on his swing so he could face her too.

"You don't look too happy about it," Tia said. She pulled her long, brown hair away from her face and swung forward to nudge him. "What's wrong?"

"She's just so damn frustrating," Conner said. "Every time we . . . you know . . . get together or whatever, she brings up Maria and gets all guilty."

"Oh, I see. So your problem is, Elizabeth has a conscience," Tia said, her eyes glowing in the darkness.

"What is it with you girls and your rules?" Conner said, kicking at the packed dirt beneath him. "Don't date a guy who your friend dated." He looked Tia in the eye. "What if the guy doesn't want the friend? What's the point?"

"You're not going to like this, but I think Elizabeth is being really smart here," Tia said, gathering up the end of the afghan and bunching it onto her lap.

"You would," Conner said.

"Seriously, Conner," Tia said. She kicked at his ankle softly to get his full attention. "Maria's been her best friend forever. Why would she trash a relationship like that when guys come and go? Especially . . ."

Conner felt his heart drop, and he tried to look Tia in the eye again, but she turned away.

"Especially what, Tee?" he asked, staring at her profile.

"Nothing," she said.

Conner's expression hardened, and he sat up straight. "Especially guys like me, right?" Conner said. "I'm not worth risking anything for because I'm a lost cause."

"Don't get all defensive, Conner," Tia said.

He stood up, flinging the swing back with a clatter. Tia reached out and grabbed it. "How could I not get defensive?" he shot back, his whisper growing hoarse.

"Jeez, Conner, look at your track record," Tia said, glaring up at him. "You're not exactly Mr. Stable."

Conner put his hands on his hips, feeling his blood boil. At least his adrenaline was warming him up. "So now I don't even get a chance to be."

Tia raised one eyebrow and smiled. "Are you saying you *want* to be?" she asked.

Conner took a step back, his heart pounding furiously. He'd said too much. He'd said things he hadn't even thought about yet. "No."

Tia stood up, clutching her colorful blanket around her shoulders as her smile widened. "I don't believe it. Conner McDermott is in lo-*ove*," she teased.

"I gotta go," Conner said, inching backward. "I don't even know why I came over here."

"I don't know—maybe because you like Elizabeth and you wanted to tell your best friend?" Tia singsonged. She was enjoying this just a little too much. Then a gut-wrenching thought occurred to Conner, and he froze in his tracks.

"You're not going to tell her about this," he said, his pulse pounding in his ears.

Tia walked up to him, the smile gone from her face. "I won't tell her about it if you don't mess it up," she said. "And if you care about Elizabeth at all, you'll let her handle the Maria thing."

"But—"

"Shhh!" She held up a hand to silence him. "Just be patient for once, Conner. Elizabeth is worth it."

Conner bowed his head and stared at the freshly cut grass as Tia's words sank in. She was right. Elizabeth's situation with Maria was really none of his business—he just hated the way it kept coming between him and Elizabeth. And he'd never admit this to anyone, including Tia, but he hated the fact that it was obviously tearing Elizabeth apart.

Conner wouldn't call that love, but it was definitely something.

"Jess?" Elizabeth whispered, silently opening the door to her sister's bedroom at the Fowlers' mansion. "Jess, wake up." She heard a tiny snore and tiptoed into the dark room, kicking piles of clothes out of the way as she went. Some things never changed no matter where they were living. "Jessica!" she stage-whispered.

"What?" Jessica said, still asleep. She rolled over and blinked a few times.

"Hey," Elizabeth said, nudging Jessica's leg.

"Oh my God!" Jessica sat straight up in bed, her hand over her chest.

"Shhh! It's just me!" Elizabeth whispered, her heart racing.

"Liz?" Jessica asked. She leaned over and turned on the light. Elizabeth squinted as the sudden brightness pierced her eyes. Jessica squinted back, then looked at the digital clock on her nightstand. "What are you doing here? How did you even get in?"

Elizabeth plopped down on Jessica's soft, queen-sized bed and shrugged. "I scaled the garden wall, climbed up the trellis to the upstairs deck, and then picked the lock. It was all very *Mod Squad*."

"Yeah, right," Jessica said with a huge yawn. She kicked at the twisted sheets and comforter, trying to smooth them out. Then she turned and fluffed the expensive feather pillows behind her.

Elizabeth laughed. "Actually, Lila let me in."

"Yeah, right," Jessica repeated, propping herself up. "That's even less believable."

"Well, you'll be happy to know I scared the life out of her," Elizabeth said. "She was getting a snack in the kitchen, and I tapped on the window. I thought she was going to pee on the floor."

Jessica smiled and stretched. "Cool. And now I'm all comfy, so what are you doing here?"

Elizabeth took a deep breath. "I have something to tell you, and I need your advice. But you have to promise not to get mad at me," she said.

"This sounds juicy," Jessica said, pushing her hair behind her ears. "Why would I get mad?"

"For not telling you about it before," Elizabeth answered. She pulled her legs up onto the bedspread and sat Indian style, facing her sister. "This thing that I'm going to tell you . . . has been going on for a while."

"Does it have anything to do with a certain Conner McDermott?" Jessica asked, raising her eyebrows.

Elizabeth's heart skipped, either from surprise or just from hearing his name. "How did you *know?*" she asked, whacking her sister's knee.

"Because I'm *me*," Jessica said, copying Elizabeth's incredulous tone. "You're so obviously into him. How could you possibly think I didn't know?"

"You never mentioned it," Elizabeth said.

"Well, neither did you," Jessica shot back. "But you're living with him, Liz! This is so against your omnipresent logic."

Elizabeth's brow furrowed. "Did you just use the word *omnipresent?*"

"I go to school too, you know," Jessica said. "So what do you need my advice about?"

"Well, let's see," Elizabeth said. "First there's the fact that he's a total jerk with no redeeming qualities, second is the whole living-with-him thing, and last but not least there's the whole lying-to-Maria-and-sneaking-around-behind-her-back-while-she-keeps-telling-me-what-a-great-friend-I-am thing." Elizabeth flopped onto her back and stared at the ceiling. "I am a horrible, horrible person."

"First of all, you are not a horrible person," Jessica said. She leaned forward, grabbed Elizabeth's wrists, and pulled her back up. Elizabeth slumped and stared at her sister. "You're just confused. So here's your wake-up call."

"I'm ready," Elizabeth said. "Hit me."

"One," Jessica said, holding up her index finger, "the living-with-him thing? Lock your door at night, shower early in the morning, never, ever walk around in that ratty flannel you like to call a nightgown, and don't do anything I wouldn't do."

Elizabeth smiled. She knew she'd come to the right place.

"Two. It doesn't matter if he doesn't have any redeeming qualities that are obvious to the world . . . I mean aside from his unfairly incredible looks," Jessica said. "If Elizabeth Wakefield likes him, there has to be something there . . . somewhere."

Elizabeth laughed. "I'll let you know when I pinpoint it."

"Please do," Jessica said. "And third, tell Maria."

"Tell Maria," Elizabeth repeated. Why did everyone keep telling her what she already knew?

"Yes, tell her," Jessica repeated, leaning back again. "Because if you don't tell her, she's either gonna read your diary, or see you kissing, or find a love note, or do something else straight out of a movie of the week, and there will be a whole big mistrust thing. . . ." Jessica paused to take a breath. "Don't make me remind you what happened when I found out about you and Ken last year."

Elizabeth shuddered. "That's the best argument I've heard yet." She smiled at Jessica. "I'll talk to Maria if you talk to Jeremy," she said.

"Yeah, well, we're working together tomorrow. He can't avoid me then," Jessica said, stretching her arms.

"Good." Elizabeth leaned forward and hugged her sister. "Thank you so much, Jess."

"Anytime," Jessica answered. Then she pulled back and looked at the clock again. "Actually, anytime other than two-thirty in the morning."

"Deal," Elizabeth said. "I'd better get going." She stood up and was overcome by a head rush that made her suddenly very tired. Blinking rapidly, Elizabeth straightened her jacket and stifled a yawn.

"Why don't you stay over?" Jessica asked. "You look exhausted, and it's practically dawn anyway."

"Thanks for the invite, but I can't," Elizabeth said with a smile. "I stole Conner's car." She pulled his keys out of her pocket and shook them.

"You did not!" Jessica exclaimed, climbing out of bed.

Elizabeth held out Conner's guitar-pick key chain as evidence.

Jessica's eyes widened. She stalked over to the window and looked out at the driveway, then spun around, her cheeks flushed. "You did! Liz, you're such the closet rebel."

Elizabeth grinned at her sister, her eyes bright. "I know. Scary, isn't it?"

TIA RAMIREZ

EVERYONE THINKS THAT ANGEL AND I FELL IN LOVE AT FIRST SIGHT. IT'S BECAUSE WE'RE SO MUSHY AND EVERYTHING. PEOPLE JUST THINK WE MUST HAVE HAD THAT WHOLE LIGHTNING-BOLT MOMENT. BUT IT'S SO NOT TRUE. ACTUALLY, WE HATED EACH OTHER.

ANGEL HAS ALWAYS BEEN VERY MATURE, AND I HAVE ALWAYS BEEN VERY . . . NOT. I'M HYPER, I RARELY EVER SHUT UP, AND I HAVE THIS HABIT OF TRICKING PEOPLE INTO DOING THINGS THEY DON'T NECESSARILY WANT TO DO. WAIT. THAT SOUNDS BAD. I JUST SORT OF NUDGE THEM IN THE DIRECTION THEY <u>SHOULD</u> BE GOING IN BECAUSE THEY DON'T REALIZE THEY SHOULD. LET ME EXPLAIN.

LIKE WITH ELIZABETH. SHE TOLD ME SHE LIKED SOME GUY, AND I KNEW IT WAS CONNER (I HAVE INTUITION ABOUT THESE THINGS—IT'S A GIFT), SO I TOLD HER TO KISS THE GUY. I KNEW THEY

SHOULD BE TOGETHER, SO I RECOMMENDED THAT ELIZABETH DO SOMETHING SHE WOULD NORMALLY NEVER DO. BUT APPARENTLY SHE DID.

ANYWAY, WAY BACK WHEN, I USED TO GET ON ANGEL'S NERVES LIKE YOU WOULD NOT BELIEVE. I REMEMBER WHEN I FIRST SAW HIM, I THOUGHT HE WAS TO DIE FOR, SO I TOLD HIM. HE JUST LOOKED SCARED AND WALKED AWAY. I THOUGHT THAT WAS PRETTY RUDE, SO I GAVE UP ON HIM. BUT THEN MY OLDER BROTHER RICKY STARTED HANGING OUT WITH ANGEL, AND HE WAS ALWAYS AROUND MY HOUSE. AND WE WERE ALWAYS IRRITATING EACH OTHER, AND THEN ONE DAY WE JUST KISSED. WE WERE ARGUING ABOUT THE UCLA-USC GAME, AND HE WAS SO MISGUIDEDLY IMPASSIONED, I JUST HAD TO KISS HIM. AND—THIS WAS A SHOCK TO ME AT THE TIME—HE KISSED ME BACK.

I THINK I JUST GREW ON HIM. JUST LIKE ELIZABETH IS GROWING ON CONNER.

ALL THANKS TO ME.

making Her Proud

By the time Jessica walked into House of Java on Sunday morning, her nerves were fried. After Elizabeth had left her room in the wee hours of the morning, she'd been obsessing about what to say to Jeremy and had barely slept five minutes. Then there was the marathon fashion show this morning, deciding which outfit sent the appropriate message.

Problem was, Jessica still wasn't quite sure what the appropriate message was.

She glanced around the cozy café, scanning the mismatched tables and secluded booths, and didn't find Jeremy. Big sigh of relief. She had a few minutes to calm herself.

"Hey, Jess," Daniel called from behind the counter. "Want a mochaccino?" He adjusted his battered baseball cap as he reached for a ceramic mug.

"No!" Jessica said, crossing the room and joining him by the milk steamer. "No coffee, no chocolate, no caffeine." She took a deep breath, and her senses filled with the pungent smell of freshly ground coffee. "If I could block my nostrils and still breathe comfortably, I would."

Daniel laughed. "All right. All right. What are you on?" he joked.

"Adrenaline," Jessica said, glancing over her shoulder as the bells by the door jangled. A pair of freshman girls walked in, giggling all the way. "Nervous adrenaline."

"Well, it looks good on you," Daniel said with a smile.

Jessica glanced down at her carefully chosen ensemble—denim shorts, light blue T-shirt, and lucky suede sneakers. "Thanks," she said. "I think." She hadn't realized her most important accessory was going to be psychotic nervousness. Too bad she hadn't known that when she was trying on her tenth outfit.

"Okay, I'll be right back," she said. Jessica pushed into the back room and almost tripped over her manager, Ally Scott.

"Sorry," Jessica said. *I have to calm down.*

"Hey, Jess," Ally greeted her, sitting down at her cluttered desk. "I like to see that kind of energy on a Sunday morning."

"I try," Jessica said, crossing the cluttered stockroom/break room to drop her bag by the coatrack. *You won't appreciate it so much when Jeremy and I get into a screaming match because I can't control myself,* she thought. Speaking of Jeremy . . .

Jessica checked the wall clock. It was five minutes to nine, so technically he wasn't late. She just wished he would get here so she could get this conversation over with. Whatever it was going to be. Grabbing a green HOJ apron, Jessica pushed back through the swinging door and out into the sunlit shop. When she saw Daniel again, she froze.

"Hey, wait a minute," Jessica said, tying her apron around her waist. "What are you doing here this morning? I thought you were working tonight."

Daniel handed a scruffy-looking, twenty-something guy his change and slammed the register drawer. "I am," he said. "Tonight, this morning, tomorrow. Just call me HOJ Man."

Jessica leaned back against the cabinets. "Why did Ally call you in, though?" she asked, glancing around the café. "It's not that busy."

"Oh, well, your boyfriend called in sick," Daniel said, his blue eyes teasing.

Jessica felt her adrenaline pumper stop pumping. She didn't even bother asking Daniel where he got the boyfriend thing from. "He did?" she asked.

"Aw. You're so cute," Daniel said, pinching her cheek. "Don't worry. I don't think it's terminal."

"Jeremy called in sick," she said, disbelieving. Jeremy never called in sick. If anyone was "HOJ Man," it was him. The guy practically lived among the cappuccino makers and grinding machines.

"Yeah. I figured you'd know since you two have been hanging out and everything," Daniel said, wiping down the counter. "Ally said he sounded totally wiped out."

He's not wiped out, Jessica thought, gripping the countertop. *He's avoiding me.* What an immature, totally ridiculous maneuver. One of the good guys? He didn't even have the guts to tell her to her face that he thought she was a loser.

"So, how was your little date on Friday night?" Daniel asked.

Jessica just looked at him, momentarily unable to form a coherent thought. Jeremy had gotten his message across loud and clear, without ever saying a word. He wasn't going to apologize. He wasn't even going to let her tell her side. How could she have been so totally wrong about him?

"Enlightening," Jessica answered finally. "Let's just leave it at that."

"Ookay," Daniel said, turning back to the counter.

Jessica clenched her fists, her adrenaline resurging for a whole new reason. Jeremy just wasn't going to get away without a confrontation. It was time for Jessica to start standing up for herself. She glanced at the neon clock behind her. She knew she was going to be counting the minutes until her shift was over. Problem was, she was working a double.

"Eight hours, Aames," she said. "Then ready or not, here I come."

On Sunday morning Jeremy woke up to the now familiar steady beeping of his father's heart monitor. The noise had ceased to annoy him and had somehow actually become comforting. It meant his father's ticker was still ticking away.

He rubbed his eyes and looked at his dad. There was a lot more color in Mr. Aames's face, and he was wearing a serene, unpained expression. Jeremy smiled slightly and leaned back in his chair. Maybe he'd just get a few more minutes' sleep.

But the moment he closed his eyes, he heard the soft clicking of his mother's steps as she entered the room. Jeremy was instantly alert.

"Jeremy, honey, I can't believe you stayed here all night," she whispered, setting a bakery bag down on the table next to his father's bed. "You look exhausted."

"I'm okay," Jeremy said, pushing himself back in the seat in an attempt to sit up straight. He reached for the white bag, which was giving off a warm, cinnamon smell. "This for me?"

Mrs. Aames smiled. "Well, I'm not going to bring your father frosted cinnamon buns," she said. "But you'd better take them outside before he wakes up and smells them."

"Good idea," Jeremy said, gingerly picking up his

breakfast as he stood. "But get me if he wakes up," he added.

"Jeremy, I want you to go home and get some rest," his mother said. "You've hardly slept in the last two days, and you have school tomorrow."

Jeremy felt his expression harden. "I'd rather stay here," he said.

"Well, I'd rather you take care of yourself," Mrs. Aames said, crossing her slim arms over her chest. Jeremy could tell her mothering instincts were as on as ever. "Making yourself sick isn't going to help your father."

Jeremy turned away from his mom. *Getting on Dad's case won't help him either,* he thought.

"Jeremy . . ."

"I said, I'll stay," Jeremy snapped.

"Hey, you two. What's all the arguing about?"

Jeremy turned at the sound of his father's groggy voice, and his mother rushed right to the bedside. "Hey, Dad!" Jeremy said brightly. "How do you feel?"

Mr. Aames blinked a few times and placed his hands flat at his sides, as if he was assessing the situation. "Better, actually," he said finally. He pushed himself up slightly and reached for the buttons to adjust his bed. Moments later he had himself in a sitting position.

He smiled at Jeremy. "What have you got there, son?" he asked. "Smells good."

"Nothing you can have," Jeremy's mother said, adjusting the pillows behind Mr. Aames's head and neck. "But I have good news. The doctor says you can come home with us this afternoon."

"Really?" Jeremy said.

"Yes. He'll be by in a few minutes to explain everything and have us sign some forms," Mrs. Aames explained.

"That *is* good news," Mr. Aames said. "I think it calls for a cinnamon bun, don't you, Jeremy?"

"Totally," Jeremy agreed. But when he took one step toward his father, his mom intercepted him.

"Jeremy's going home to get some rest," Mrs. Aames said, taking a firm hold on his arm.

"No, I'm not," Jeremy said, unthrilled with the whine in his voice.

"Outside, Jeremy," she said, leveling him with a just-try-me stare. "Now." His shoulders slumped, and he trudged toward the door, his mother following close behind.

"Sorry, Dad," he said.

"Hey! Your mom's a tough one," Mr. Aames called after him.

Out in the hallway Jeremy turned on his mother, squaring his shoulders defensively. He had at least six inches on the woman—maybe he could intimidate her into letting him stay. But one look at his mother's livid expression turned him into a five-year-old again.

"I know what you're doing, Jeremy," she accused. "You're trying to protect your father from me."

"Mom—"

"What do you think of me?" she asked, sorrow mixing with the anger in her voice. "Do you really think I would risk his health by upsetting him?"

"But you said—"

"Yes, I said your father has to get a job," Mrs. Aames whispered. "But I don't expect him to walk out of here and straight into a cubicle. I'm fully aware that this is a conversation for another time."

Jeremy put his hands on his hips and sighed at the floor. He felt like the weight of everything that had happened over the past two days was crushing him, grinding him into the spotless linoleum. But above all he just felt guilty. His mom had already been through so much. The last thing she needed was mistrust from her son.

"I'm sorry, Mom," he said quietly, still staring at the floor.

She reached out and took his hand. "I know you're just trying to protect him too. But you don't have to protect him from me," she said, pressing her thumb into his palm. Her fingers felt so small and delicate against his skin, and Jeremy wondered how anyone who looked so fragile could be so strong. Strong enough to keep the family going for a year while his father withered away.

Jeremy leaned over and wrapped his arms

around his mother. "I'm really sorry," he said again.

She patted him on the back. "It's going to be okay," she said into his shoulder. "I promise." She broke away and tilted her head back to look at him. "But only if you go home and get directly into bed."

Jeremy smiled. "How about if I go home, set things up for Dad, call someone I should have called hours ago, and then get directly into bed?"

"Stubborn as ever," Mrs. Aames said, returning his smile. "Are you calling the girl I forced you to abandon at Trent's on Friday night?" she asked.

Jeremy felt as if his heart were being squeezed inside a huge fist. *Abandon* was the perfect word, although his mother couldn't have known it since she hadn't heard the whole drama-filled story. But for the first time since this ordeal with his father started, Jeremy realized the full gravity of the situation. Jessica probably thought he was the most heartless, worthless guy in the world.

"Mom? I gotta go," Jeremy said, as if they hadn't been discussing that very topic ever since she had arrived.

He kissed her quickly on the cheek and took off down the ICU hallway at a jog. "Tell Dad I'll see him later at home!" he called over his shoulder. He had to get Jessica on the phone as soon as possible. He only hoped she would listen to what he had to say.

*   *   *

Elizabeth placed her coffee mug down next to the Sunday newspaper she had spread out over the kitchen table. She was already on to her second cup, but neither the caffeine dose nor the cold shower she'd taken had done much to get her blood flowing. Now she was just a clean zombie with coffee breath.

"That's the last time I take a dead-of-night field trip to the Fowlers'," she mumbled, falling into her chair. She stared at the words going in and out of focus on the newspaper. Usually Elizabeth spent Sunday morning trying to learn something new about the world, but that was obviously not happening today. Folding her arms across the paper, she dropped her head and yawned.

"Mind if I join you?"

Elizabeth raised her face just enough to make eye contact with Megan, who was looking annoyingly awake. Her strawberry blond hair was neatly braided, and her green eyes actually seemed alive. "Be my guest," Elizabeth said.

"Thanks," Megan mumbled as she dumped an armload of books on the table, then sighed melodramatically.

"History paper?" Elizabeth asked, eyeing Megan's books.

"Yep. It's a total nightmare." She picked up her open notebook and read, "'Write a five-page paper on the Industrial Revolution and the effect of standardized parts.'" Megan narrowed her eyes at Elizabeth. "What's a standardized part?"

"Huh," Elizabeth said, squinting. "I feel like I should know that. Is it for Mr. Lewinter?"

Megan nodded as she flipped through her huge history book. "Standardized parts. Standardized parts," she repeated as she ran a finger over the detailed contents. "Oh, I remember! It's, like, screws and nuts and bolts and stuff. Ugh."

"That sounds like fun," Elizabeth said sarcastically.

"I'm doomed," Megan wailed.

The phone rang, and Megan jumped for it. "Saved by the bell," she said. "You think it's the history gods, offering to do this for me?"

"That would be nice," Elizabeth said, covering her mouth as she yawned again.

Megan picked up the phone. "Hello? Yeah. She's right here." She held the telephone out to Elizabeth. "Not the history gods."

Elizabeth smiled at Megan sympathetically and took the receiver. "Hello?"

"Hey, Liz." It was Maria.

Elizabeth sighed. "Hey."

"You sound like I feel."

Elizabeth answered with a noncommittal grunt. Megan moaned and dropped her head onto her notebook.

"Actually," Elizabeth said, "neither of us sounds even remotely as pathetic as Megan. She has a history paper for Lewinter."

"Oooh, one of his three-month-long assignments on a concept?" Maria asked.

"She has to write on standardized parts."

Megan moaned again.

"Ouch," Maria said. "Please pass on my condolences. If it's any consolation, I have to write a five-pager justifying a Nobel Prize for physics or chemistry or something like that by Wednesday, and I haven't even picked my topic."

"Jeez, Maria," Elizabeth said. "That sucks."

"You don't know the half of it. My modem went down this morning, and I can't even get on-line to do the research."

"Oh. Well, mine is okay," Elizabeth said. "Do you want me to bring my PowerBook over?" *And maybe while I'm there, I can tell you a little something I've been meaning to tell you for a while.*

"You don't have your car," Maria reminded her.

"That's right," Elizabeth said, leaning her forehead on her hand. *But I'm now experienced in grand theft auto. . . .*

"Why don't I come over there?" Maria asked.

Elizabeth's heart dropped. As if in answer to Maria's question, there was a loud thump above Elizabeth's head. Conner.

"Um . . . do you really think that's a good idea?" Elizabeth asked, looking at the ceiling. "I mean, Conner's here and—"

"You know what? I've decided not to care,"

Maria said. "Conner's not going to scare me away from hanging with my best friend. I'll be there in ten minutes."

"Maria, I really think . . ." Elizabeth trailed off as she heard the dial tone kick in. She stood and hung up the phone, trying to clear her groggy head. This was going to work out . . . somehow. She could just tell Maria what was going on when she got here. It was time to face the music.

There was another loud thump from upstairs. Of course, if Conner walked into the room half dressed while Elizabeth and Maria were talking, that might make things a little bit harder. And if Elizabeth had learned one thing in the few weeks she'd been staying here, it was that she could never predict when Conner was going to walk in on her.

"Where are you going?" Megan asked as Elizabeth headed for the door. "I need help."

"Just give me five minutes," Elizabeth said, bolting for the stairs. Five minutes to convince Conner to get the heck out of here before Maria showed up.

Elizabeth rushed to Conner's bedroom and knocked on the door.

"Yeah?" came the reply.

"Can I come in? I need to talk to you," Elizabeth said.

The door swung open, and Elizabeth's breath caught in her throat. Conner was standing inches away from her, wearing nothing but a faded pair of

155

baggy blue sweatpants. Why did the sight of his bare chest always render her speechless?

"Get a good look?" Conner said, leaning against the doorjamb with a crooked smile.

"Listen," Elizabeth said, ignoring his comment and opting to look into his eyes. Far less dangerous territory. "Maria's coming over here, and I'm going to talk to her about . . . you know—" She fluttered her hand in front of her, searching for her missing speech skills.

"Us?" Conner supplied.

"Yeah," Elizabeth finished gratefully.

"Good," he said, turning and walking into his room. He grabbed a T-shirt from the floor and pulled it over his head. Elizabeth was half relieved, half disappointed that he'd felt the need to get dressed.

"Right, it is good," she said, hovering near the door. "But I was wondering if . . . maybe you could . . . I don't know . . . go over to Tia's or something? Just while she's here?"

Conner looked at her, his green eyes sharp. "Tell me if I have this straight," he said slowly. "You're asking me to get out of my own house because Maria's coming over."

"Well," she hedged, her heart pounding furiously. "Yes."

Silence.

"No," Conner said flatly. He grabbed a laundry

basket out of the corner and started flinging random pieces of clothing into it, keeping his back to Elizabeth.

"Conner, I just think that while I talk to her, it would be better if you weren't around," Elizabeth explained, watching him closely.

"You are not throwing me out of my own house, Liz," he said, whipping a shirt at the basket and missing by a mile. He turned to her, his hands on his hips. "Just deal with it."

Elizabeth felt herself deflate. "Fine. I'm sorry I asked," she said. "You're right. This is your house, and it's not like I have the right to ask for anything. It's not like I *mean* anything."

She turned around and headed down the hall to her own room. Her eyes blurred over from tears and exhaustion as her emotions jumbled themselves inside her. She was angry at him for being so harsh, angry at herself for asking him to do something so idiotic, and ashamed that she'd lost her cool. It wasn't until she was halfway across her room that she realized he had followed her.

"Maria and I will just go back to her place," Elizabeth said, shoving her feet into her sneakers and keeping her back to him. "I'm sorry I—" *Shut up*, she told herself. *You sound like an idiot.*

"Liz . . ."

Shaking, she quickly and carelessly wound up her computer cords and stuffed them into her carry case.

"Liz, stop." His voice was completely transformed. Calm. Low. She turned to look at him.

"Talk to Maria, okay?" he said. "I'll just . . . stay in my room or something."

Elizabeth's heart melted along with her anger. She knew it was hard for Conner to give in . . . even just an inch. "Yeah?" she said.

"Yeah. I won't even play my guitar."

On impulse, Elizabeth crossed the room and threw her arms around Conner's neck. "Thanks," she said. Conner squeezed her back for a split second and then moved away.

"But you're gonna tell her," Conner said.

"Yeah," Elizabeth replied, her heart racing from nervous dread. "You and Jessica were both right. If I don't tell her now, she's going to find out some other way."

Maria had almost found out already when she'd seen Elizabeth's poem. The sneaking and lying had to stop. She just hoped she could find the right words to keep from breaking Maria's heart. Again.

Melissa shakily placed the empty prescription bottle on top of her dresser. She took a moment to stare at herself in the mirror. Her hair was pulled back in a neat, low ponytail, and her face was perfectly clean—free of all makeup. She was surprised by how young she looked. Young and red eyed, but determined.

The pills were in a pile in the middle of her bed-spread. If her parents had been home, she would have kept them hidden in the pocket of her light pink robe, but she didn't have to. Her parents were out. They'd come home late last night and headed out early this morning for their weekly brunch/tennis match at the country club. Melissa had heard the whole thing. She'd been sitting up in her room, counting and recounting the pills. They hadn't even checked in on her.

So her parents were out once again. And that was fine. It meant Melissa could take her time. Last time she had rushed it, and that was how it had all gone wrong.

That was why she was here now, feeling this mind-numbing pain. Rejected. Destroyed. Unloved. Pathetic.

"Pathetic," she said aloud. It was actually pathetic that her mother thought she could hide her sleeping pills from Melissa. It was even more pathetic that there were sleeping pills in the house at all. After the last time, any real parent would have stopped buying them. Any real parent would have protected her daughter at all costs. Tried warm milk or counting sheep to get to sleep.

"But not my mom," Melissa said. "My mom never changes for anyone."

Melissa perched on the edge of her bed and rolled each pill out from the pile one by one, lining them up in a perfect row.

There were twenty-seven of them. Little white-and-lime-green capsules. The dosage said two. Take two before bed.

"Or take all before breakfast," Melissa said flatly. She stared out her window at the bright blue sky, feeling as if the day was mocking her. Melissa had always hated the morning. It meant there was another day to face. Another day full of overwhelming disappointments.

But there had been one morning she liked. One she'd spent with Will. It was last year, after the junior prom. They had spent all night partying with friends and then driven to a secluded beach together to watch the sunrise. He had lain down on their blanket with his head in her lap. And as she'd brushed his soft, blond hair with her fingertips, he'd said she was the most beautiful girl he had ever seen and that this was a sunrise he'd remember forever.

"You'll remember me forever too, Will," Melissa whispered. She swiped the pills into her hand and stood slowly, grabbing the water bottle from her bedside table. Then she paused and looked out her bedroom window again, wistfully gazing at her climbing tree, and the driveway where she'd played hopscotch when she was little, and the rosebush where they'd taken their pictures before the prom.

If only she'd known then . . .

Silently Melissa left her room and crossed the hall. The house was completely still. She tiptoed into the bathroom, gently shutting the door behind her. Then she sank to the floor, her back against the wall, and unclenched her hand.

There were the pills, pressed into her sweaty, red palm. Melissa briefly considered shoving them all in her mouth and getting it over with, but she had to take her time. Last time she'd done it quickly, and she hadn't realized she'd dropped a few pills and left a few in her pocket. This time she had to take them all.

As Melissa placed the first pill in her mouth and took a sip of water, her mind flashed on an image of her mother finding her here. It would just be getting dark out. *Mom will still be in her tennis outfit,* Melissa thought. She imagined her mother dropping to the floor on her bare knees, yelling at Melissa to wake up. Yelling about what Melissa had done. Why was she so ungrateful? Why was she always doing everything wrong?

Well, Mom, this is one thing I'm going to get right, Melissa thought as she popped her next pill. *Maybe for once you'll be proud.*

melissa Fox

"Dear Will, I hope you and Jessica are very happy. . . ."

"Dear Will, When you left me after the football game, I was so lonely. . . ."

"Dear Will, I apologize ahead of time for any inconveniences this may have caused. . . ."

"Dear Will, Please don't blame yourself. . . ."

"Dear Will, I love you. I . . ."

"Dear Will, How can I explain. . . ."

"Dear Will, By the time you read this . . ."

"Dear Will, Please don't think this is your fault. . . ."

"Dear mom,"

"Dear Will,"

Oh, forget it.

CHAPTER
Maybe Never
10

Jessica checked the address she had scrawled on the napkin and looked back at the house—no, mansion—no, *palace* in front of her. The place was huge. Her heart sank.

"This has got to be wrong," she said, checking the napkin again. Nope, the addresses matched. The place was considerably bigger than Fowler Crest. So Jeremy was a millionaire. No wonder he was acting like such a snob. Country Club Boy probably couldn't handle his friends thinking he was dating a notorious slut.

Jessica imagined herself walking up to that huge, wooden door, and her courage fled. She almost threw the Jeep into reverse. Almost. But she knew she'd never forgive herself if she backed down now. She killed the engine and twisted the rearview mirror toward her so she could check her face.

"Go," she instructed her reflection as she fluffed her hair. "Don't let him get away with blowing you off."

Jessica climbed out of the Jeep, took a deep breath, and shook back her hair. She was so nervous, she barely registered the long trek up to the door before she was ringing the bell. She pressed the button and waited.

"This house is so big, the butler probably needs a golf cart just to get to the door," she muttered.

At that moment the door swung open and Jeremy stood there in a clingy blue T-shirt, freshly showered and looking *way* too fine.

But Jessica was determined to stay focused. She would not look into those big brown eyes.

Too late. "Uh . . ."

"Jessica!" Jeremy exclaimed with a big, surprised smile. "I just left you a message. What are you . . ." He trailed off and looked behind him into the house. "What are you doing here?" he asked apprehensively. He was suddenly uncomfortable. Cute, but uncomfortable.

Yeah, right, you left me a message, Jessica thought. "I came over to see how you were feeling," she said with exaggerated false sympathy. "I heard you were sick this morning."

"I'm . . . um . . . I'm not sick," he said with a nervous laugh. He was still holding on to the door as if he was ready to slam it in her face.

"I didn't think so," Jessica said.

"Listen, Jess, I'm really glad you came over, and I would invite you in, but now's not really a good time—"

"No?" Jessica interrupted, crossing her arms over

166

her chest. His stammering was helping her regain her courage. "Well, that's fine because I can say what I need to say right here."

Jeremy paled. "Jessica, wait a second—"

But Jessica was ready to burst, and nothing was stopping her. "I can't believe that you just believed what those girls said about me at that party," Jessica fumed. "I can't believe you let me run out of there all humiliated and didn't even come after me to see if I was okay. I can't believe you care so much about your stupid image that you would do that to me."

"I don't care about my image," Jeremy said.

"Really?" Jessica snapped, her voice rising. "You sure fooled me. You know, just because your life is so perfect, that doesn't give you the right to treat other people like dirt. To treat *me* like dirt. And I . . . I . . ."

Jessica paused for breath. A very small voice inside her suggested that perhaps she should save some of her rage for the others who deserved it. There was the small matter of Melissa, Will, Cherie, Gina, Lila, and the entire population of SVH.

"Are you finished?" Jeremy asked.

"What?" she said sharply.

"Are you finished?" he repeated. "Because I wouldn't want to interrupt."

Jessica narrowed her eyes at him. He was mocking her, but she wasn't going to be completely immature about this whole thing. In fact, she was pretty much dying to know what his excuse could be.

"Go ahead," Jessica said. "Interrupt."

Jeremy eyed her for a second, as if he was gauging her temper and deciding whether it was safe to proceed. "You know what?" he said finally. "Why don't you come inside? I have something to show you." He took a step back and held the door open for her.

Where is he going with this? Jessica wondered. "Fine, but you only have five seconds," she said, stepping inside. She sucked in her breath. The place was nearly empty and strangely cold. "Where's the furniture?"

"Gone. Sold. We sold it weeks ago. Want to see more of my 'perfect world'? Follow me." He led her past a huge, completely empty room and down a hall into a large, sparsely decorated kitchen.

"This is where we live, Jessica. In this kitchen, in three bedrooms—one for my parents, one for me, and one for my sisters—and this family room right here."

They walked into another modestly decorated room. There was a worn leather couch with the Hide-a-Bed pulled out and neatly made up, a coffee table, a thin rug, and a big-screen TV that dwarfed the rest of the furnishings.

"Why is the bed out?" she asked in a quiet voice. Suddenly she felt very small. Small and totally out of line.

"Jess," he said, his voice stressed out and thin. "My father had a heart attack on Friday. The bed is for him."

Jessica's hand flew up to cover her mouth. "Oh my God."

"That's why I didn't—couldn't go after you at the party," Jeremy continued, his voice gaining strength. "Well, I did, but I only got as far as the driveway. My mom pulled up as you were running off. I've spent the entire weekend hanging out with the ICU nurses, listening to machines beep all over my father because he was so stressed out over the fact that he hasn't had a job in more than a year that he stressed himself right into a choice room at Joshua Fowler Memorial Hospital."

"Oh, Jeremy," Jessica said quietly, her heart aching. "I'm so sorry. I can't believe I—"

"It's okay," Jeremy said, leaning against the back of the couch. "You didn't know."

"How is he?" Jessica asked.

"He's doing better," Jeremy said, rubbing the back of his neck with his palm. "He's coming home this afternoon, but he's going to need someone to take care of him, and we won't be able to afford a duty nurse." He pushed away from the couch and slowly walked across the room to the back window. "I'm going to have to do a lot of it."

"Can you do that?" Jessica asked. "I mean, you've got school . . . and—"

"And work and football," Jeremy interrupted. He turned to her, a kind of defiant desperation in his eyes. "I already take care of everything, Jessica. Everything. My sisters, meals, the house, the lawn, the gutters. I need an eighteen-foot ladder just to change a freakin' lightbulb. I take care of the checkbook and all the bill collectors. And my after-school job? Most of that money goes toward groceries." He paused to take several deep breaths. "Still think my life is so perfect?"

Jessica walked up to him and tried to take his hand in hers, but it felt wooden. "Jeremy, I am so sorry. I feel like such an idiot. I didn't . . . I didn't know."

As the full weight of what Jeremy had told her washed over her, Jessica suddenly felt like a total whiner. Jeremy was a seventeen-year-old ball of responsibility, and she was upset that a bunch of spineless morons had trashed her reputation?

Jeremy squeezed her hand. "You want to know what I know?"

"What?" Jessica said meekly.

"I know that nothing those girls said about you matters. True or not, it would never matter—you know why?"

She just shook her head, too overwhelmed by sorrow and confusion to say anything.

Jeremy slid his arms around her shoulders. "None of it matters because I like the Jessica Wakefield I know."

Jessica's eyes filled with tears.

"And the few times that I've been with you . . . it's like I've actually forgotten about all that other stuff," he said, his deep brown eyes searching hers.

It was a good thing Jeremy was holding her because she almost collapsed. She felt his fingers under her chin, lifting, and then suddenly his lips touched hers, and nothing mattered anymore.

Nothing mattered but Jeremy.

Elizabeth leaned closer to her mirror and applied her lipstick with a fluttering hand. She didn't exactly need makeup to talk to Maria, but at least it was keeping Elizabeth busy. If she went over her speech one more time, she was going to drive herself crazy.

Out of the corner of her eye she saw Conner walk past her open door, then heard his footsteps on the stairs. He'd changed into jeans and a flannel. Maybe he actually *was* going out. Elizabeth dropped the open lipstick on her desk and ran into the hallway.

"Where are you going?" Elizabeth asked.

Conner stopped halfway down the staircase and looked up at her. "I'm going to the kitchen to get something to eat," he said. "Or is that not allowed?"

Elizabeth closed her eyes and willed herself to stay calm. *Count to ten. It's going to be okay.* "One . . . two," she began as she slowly descended the stairs. But when she hit the foyer she abandoned the destressing techniques and practically ran to the kitchen. Conner was bent over the refrigerator, scanning the shelves. Megan had taken her books to her room, and Mrs. Sandborn had left for some country-club thing fifteen minutes earlier. Why was Conner the only person who refused to disappear?

She breathed a sigh of relief as he reached into the refrigerator and came out with a bottle of iced tea.

"Okay, you've got something," she said, walking up behind him and pulling on the belt loops of his jeans. "Let's go."

Conner peeled her fingers from his pants and chuckled. "I said I was hungry, not thirsty," he said, sauntering over to the walk-in pantry. Even his walk was mercilessly slow.

"She's going to be here any minute," Elizabeth said, following him in desperate frustration.

Conner turned to her, a mischievous smile in his eyes. "Then we'd better hide," he said in a teasing, yet perfectly serious voice. He grabbed her wrist and pulled her into the pantry, attempting to close the door behind them in one motion.

Elizabeth's heart was pounding in her ears, but she managed to stop the door with her foot. It slammed against her sneaker and flew open with a bang.

Conner grinned at her. "Okay. We can do this

with the door open," he said. He put the bottle of iced tea down on a shelf, and before Elizabeth knew it, he'd slipped both hands under her hair and was cupping her cheeks. Her entire body was shivering.

"Conner—"

But he didn't let her finish. He kissed her once, softly, tenderly, and then pulled back. Elizabeth's eyes fluttered open, even though she hadn't been aware that they'd closed. For a moment she just stared at him, trying to read his ever unreadable emotions. Then he leaned in again, and Elizabeth was just about to melt into his arms when she heard the gasp.

Startled, Elizabeth pulled back and slammed right into the pantry shelves, knocking boxes and jars to the floor. But she barely noticed because her eyes were trained on one horrifying, unbelievably heartrending sight.

Maria was standing at the window of the kitchen door, and she was crying.

Jessica turned down Santa Marina Boulevard and concentrated on remembering the next side street. She'd only driven this route once in her life, and it was certainly not something she'd planned on doing again. But now she was on a mission—a mission she'd decided to take the moment she'd kissed Jeremy good-bye on the front step.

She glanced at her reflection in the rearview mirror and was pleased with the determination she saw reflected in her eyes. Jessica had taken Will on. She had taken Jeremy on—even though it had turned out she didn't have to—and now there was one more person to deal with. It was amazing how a little happiness had cleared her mind.

Just a short time ago Jessica had felt like she'd be abused and wallowing in the dregs of depression forever. But now it was obvious to her that she could control her future. And her future was not going to include Melissa Fox.

"There it is," Jessica said with a smile as Melissa's house came into view. She sat up straight in her seat, pleased with her sense of direction and almost giddy with anticipation of telling Melissa off. Jessica was going to hit that ringleader with everything she had . . . and then some.

She pulled the Jeep to a stop at the edge of the driveway and slammed the door behind her. She wanted to announce her presence—make Melissa look out the window and squirm. With a purposeful, confident stride, Jessica marched up the Foxes' front door and reached for the bell.

But just before she touched it, the door swung open.

Jessica was so startled, she jumped backward. "Will?"

Will Simmons's eyes were wide with shocked

fear. Jessica had never seen anyone look quite that stricken before.

"Will, what's wrong?" Jessica asked, frightened by his rigid demeanor.

"What the hell are you doing here?" he demanded.

"I'm here to talk to Melissa," Jessica said tentatively. The determination was gone, dispelled by Will's freak-show vibe.

"You can't."

"Why not?"

"Because you can't," Will snapped. "Go away, Jessica. You really shouldn't be here."

Jessica was about to let her temper flare up again when she heard a voice from inside the house.

"Who's at the door, Will?" A frail female voice. Too old to be Melissa's.

Will shot Jessica a look of warning—a look that threw her off. "Um, just a friend of Melissa's, Mrs. Fox. Don't worry about it."

Jessica laughed. "A friend? Are you kidding?"

Will came out onto the porch, jostling her back a few feet, and shut the door behind him.

"Shut up, Jessica," he hissed.

"What the hell is going on, Will?" Jessica asked, her pulse roaring in her ears. There was something very strange here. Something almost eerie.

Will raked his hand through his hair and looked skyward, taking a long, deep breath. Then his chin dropped down again and he looked Jessica directly in the eyes.

"You won't be talking to Melissa anytime soon, Jessica. Maybe never."

Jessica's face went slack, and her skin turned ice cold. Somehow she knew what was coming before Will ever said the words.

"Melissa's in the hospital. She tried to commit suicide this morning."

Poor Melissa.

No, I mean it. Poor Melissa.

What could have been going on in her mind? What could have made her do this? I mean, sure, she's a little out there . . . making up rumors and trying to get me kicked off the squad, but in general she's on top of the world. She has a boyfriend who obviously loves her, as much as it irritates me to say it. She's smart and pretty and talented. And she has a beautiful house. . . .

But I guess everyone has their problems, right?

Everyone has their secrets.

MARIA SLATER
7:50 P.M.

I was standing at the back door because I chickened out.

I didn't know how to act around Conner, so I thought maybe I could sneak through the back and go up to Elizabeth's room and I'd have a better chance of avoiding him.

Good plan, Maria. Good plan.

JEREMY AAMES
12:01 A.M.

I meant it when I said Jessica was the only thing in this world that helps me forget . . . the rest of this world. If I could spend all my time with her, I would. I would drop football, my job, my schoolwork . . . okay, maybe not my family. Maybe. Just kidding.

My point is, I'm going to work Jessica Wakefield into my insane life. I'm gonna squeeze in dates between practices and shifts at HOJ. I'm gonna take her out for breakfast at 8 A.M. on Sunday before my dad and sisters wake up. I'm gonna skip school and kidnap her and take her on a road trip.

Somehow I'm going to figure out a way to be with Jessica. I've always known she was worth it. And after that kiss . . . Man, is she worth it.

Complications. Just what I needed. Even more complications.

Now theres gonna be a whole "I-should-have-told-her" thing. And a whole "How-could-you-do-this-to-me?" thing. Elizabeths gonna be all distraught, and Marias going to perfect her look of death.

Complications.

Whatever Tia says, no girl is worth it.

Check out the **all-new**....

Sweet Valley Web site—

www.sweetvalley.com

New Features

Cool Prizes

The **ONLY** official Web site!

Hot Links

And much more!